THE GLORIETA PASS

CHRIS O'GRADY

The following work is a work of fiction. Names, characters, places, and incidents either are the product of the author's imagination or are used fictitiously. Any resemblance to actual persons, living or dead, events, or locales is entirely coincidental.

The Glorieta Pass

Published by
Twit Publishing
Dallas, Texas

Edited by Chris Gabrysch
Cover design by Chris Gabrysch and Neither Noir
with special thanks to Frank Horak and Brit Schulte

ISBN-13 978-0-9845477-8-4

This is for Liz, Bill, and JS.

Grazia, Tutti!

CHAPTER ONE

The wall phone at the end of the bar was giving Wilder nothing but a string of buzzes. Either Milo was out or he wasn't answering. There was no reason for him not to answer his phone and he shouldn't be out, even if Wilder was a day late. Milo should be sitting on that phone.

Tired of listening to the buzzing, Wilder hung up in disgust and returned to his drink on the bar. He was up on his barstool, lifting his glass, before he noticed the newcomer farther along the bar.

She was a dark-haired looker in a black silk dress. She sat with her legs crossed. A long length of thigh showed above the tops of sheer black stockings. Her skin appeared dead white against the black sheen of the silk skirt.

Wilder gave her more than the usual look over. She hadn't been there when he'd come in awhile back, so she must have arrived while he was on the phone.

He didn't let himself take in the display too long. This was no time for him to make any kind of pass at local stuff, not the night before pulling a job in a town he didn't know at all. And there was no sense looking at the goods unless you were going to try for some.

A couple of hours ago when he'd hit Thomaston, Wilder had been in a rush to make contact with Milo. Now it was starting to look like he was in for a long wait before he got any answers from Milo's phone.

He took another pull at his drink.

He was seated near the back end of the bar where it bent in toward the wall, leaving a gap for the barkeep to get out at that end. Absently, he glanced at the dark-haired woman again, but he was wondering how long Milo was going to keep him hung up like this. The girl in black was easy for him to see without being obvious about it, so he watched her.

She had that look, the hot-to-go look: heavy on the makeup, lots of dark guck around the eyes, pale lipstick, almost as pale as her white skin, making her mouth appear more naked than it would have with no lipstick at all.

She sat erect, her forearms resting on the edge of the bar, her fingertips just touching her glass. She stared steadily at the rows of bottles in the back of the bar, but she still looked all strung out. Every ten seconds, she would snap no-ashes from the end of her cigarette.

But there weren't any takers!

The stag hotshots up near the front would slide sneaky knowing glances back at her from where they had posted themselves along the bar. One of them even leaned way back so he could see more of her legs. But when he straightened, he just turned again to his lush buddies and they all had their laugh.

Along the wall across from the bar, couples in booths darted quick glances at her too, and there were small secret smiles and low-spoken comments.

But still no takers.

Wilder looked her over again.

She could be a hooker, except she didn't look tired enough, or brassy enough. That didn't mean a thing, though. She might still be so new at it that none of the signs stuck out yet.

The only thing Wilder kept getting from her was an itch, low and deep inside, each time he looked over at her sitting there. That was usually the only message he needed.

Not tonight, though.

Deliberately, he swung his eyes away from her and concentrated on his drink. He need to wait and give Milo enough time to get back to his phone. Wilder could feel the impatience starting to build inside, even though he knew there was a good enough reason why Milo wasn't hanging around his phone waiting for his call: Wilder was a day late.

He'd been due up here in Thomaston last night, but there had been one more run of good luck to find out about in a floating crap game. He'd stuck with the luck until it petered out. When it was gone altogether and he knew his luck was still bad, he had rented a car and headed north. He'd have to pull the gambling joint stickup Milo had fingered.

Wilder had come up the highway from the south after spending the afternoon checking out secondary roads, in case he needed alternate getaway routes after the job. Just after dark, he'd reached Thomaston's outlying districts. When the first skyscraper lights had appeared above the horizon ahead, he'd stopped at a roadside phone booth next to a gas station to call Milo. He didn't have Milo's address, and he couldn't look it up in the local phone book because he didn't know his last name.

It didn't matter. Usually in deals like this, all he needed was a phone number. Except this time nobody was answering any phones. *Why doesn't the jerk get an answering machine?* Wilder thought.

Driving on along the highway, he'd passed a sign that said City Limit and gave the population. Getting himself a motel room, he'd taken a quick shower and went out to eat. When he got through with supper, he'd tried the phone again. Still no answer. Driving back to his motel, he stopped in this bar for a drink and tried Milo's number again, without success. By then, he knew he was in for a long evening of waiting and phoning.

Nursing his drink, Wilder wondered if his luck was completely gone. If it was, he might do himself a favor if he sheered off the gambling joint heist Milo had set up for tomorrow night. If his luck was really out, he wouldn't get away with the grab, no matter how well he planned it.

Like tonight. He shouldn't have had to get a motel room. Right now, he should be jungled up at Milo's place, where no cops and no one could lay an eye on him and maybe remember afterward, from out of nowhere, that they had seen him making the scene around town.

Not that a gambling setup was like a bank. Still, a grab was a grab. Cops want you no matter whom you steal from.

If gambling was going on in this town, they'd have a fix in with the law somewhere up the ladder. Which meant that after he pulled the job, there would be some looking for whoever did it. Maybe a lot of looking. The cops would check out recent arrivals in all the hotels and motels. And that meant he might even have to drop the Wilder name and start using another phony one.

Thinking of all that disgusted Wilder. Too many things were beginning to look bad, even before he got started. Especially that name change. He wasn't crazy about that possibility.

He shook his head. It was too much trouble for too small a money return. How much could you hit a gambling layout for in a city this size?

Ah, hell! He was doing too much thinking about it.

Quit the thinking, he told himself. He wasn't living this way so he could die of old age, anyway. Time for another crack at the phone. Spinning around on the stool, he hit the floor, and headed for the phone. When he tried Milo's number again and the same old buzzing kept up, Wilder cursed under his breath.

He could see the broad in the black silk dress, still perched on her barstool. Wilder knew damn well he shouldn't go near any woman the night before pulling a job . . . but the way he was feeling now, he'd either get rid of it with a woman or before the night was done he'd wind up breaking someone's jaw.

When he knew the buzzing was just going to go on and on, he slammed the receiver down on the hook.

Okay, screw Milo. And the gambling joint. The job was jinxed, so forget it.

He went back to his drink on the bar.

When the bartender came down to his end of the bar again, Wilder told him, “Give the lady there whatever she’s drinking.”

The bartender squinted at him, then down at the folded over fiver lying just beyond his fingertips.

“You sure you want to make a pass at her, mister? That woman is married. And to a very prominent citizen of our city, if you know what I mean.”

Wilder shrugged. “They’re always married.”

The barman tilted his head resignedly. “Okay,” he murmured, “so I mind my own business.”

The fiver disappeared. Easing along behind the bar, the barkeep leaned across it to the woman and spoke softly to her. She glanced at Wilder. Her dark eyes flashed angrily. Her mouth tightened. But after a moment, she nodded and said something. The barkeep put a fresh drink on the bar in front of her, then took his time polishing a glass while he drifted back to Wilder, where he picked up another two dollars for the woman’s drink.

“The lady thanks you,” he said. A small wicked look gleamed in his eye, but his face remained bland.

Wilder nodded.

Finishing the drink he was on, he watched the bottles on the shelves for a few beats. Then he got up and went along the bar and took the stool next to the woman’s.

“Quiet night, so far,” he observed, not looking at her. From the corner of his eye, he could see her head turn.

The barman came over. Wilder knocked his knuckles on the bar for the same thing he’d been drinking before.

“It’ll pick up,” she said. “Give it time.”

Her voice was thin, ragged sounding, as if she was trying not to put too much weight into it when she spoke.

“How much time?”

“Not too much.”

But she hadn't kept the leash on her voice tight enough. There was a muted shriek in it, a scratchy sound she had been trying to control. The sound was a giveaway.

Wilder turned his head and looked directly at her. Coal-black hair. Full pale lips in a white-skinned face. Skin stretched too taut over the cheekbones.

Her teeth were clenched. The jaw muscles bulged slightly. Her eyes swung toward him and watched him with a far horizon look in them, but now Wilder realized she wasn't seeing him at all. She wasn't seeing anything. Instead, she was listening to the long, sad, hopeless song her body was singing inside her.

Maybe she was wondering when the endless song would stop and give her peace, and not force her to sit at bars like this. Where anyone could watch a guy like himself come along and start moving the verbal chess pieces, and she would be forced to go along with it or the fierce hot animal inside her would tear her to shreds.

"Not too much time," she added harshly, "but some. That's important."

She looked bitter. Her lips quivered loosely, then they were still once more. She wanted him to work it right.

Wilder wondered whether he should bother. Tonight, he was feeling impatient. He didn't want to work anything by the book. He just wanted to get to it, a quick piece, then on his way.

He was beginning to wish he'd hunted up a real hooker, somewhere downtown, instead of bothering with this one. He watched her, curious. The muscles in her throat jerked. She was stretched as tight as a drum skin.

Wilder didn't like it. She might turn out to be trouble. With his luck running like it was lately, even a little trouble might be way too much.

Alright, he was here, and the routine was already under way, so he made an effort to handle it nice and polite. He pushed the guff out and waited for her answers. When they came, they were short, harsh, breathless, and getting more ragged by the second.

Finally, Wilder thought the hell with the slow way. Reaching over, he put the palm of his hand on her forearm where it rested on the edge of the bar.

The woman went rigid. Her jaw tightened again. She didn't look at Wilder. Her head reared up and she stared fixedly in front of her. The breath whistled in her nostrils, she sucked it in so fast.

Wilder kept watching her and he kept his hand on her arm.

Come on, he was thinking irritably, *settle down, sister.*

It hung that way for several beats, with the woman sitting bolt upright, her eyes wide and staring, her face stern and furious, holding her breath. Then her jaw abruptly unclamped. Her lips softened, parted. Her eyes began to close. Wilder could barely hear her soft sigh, "Ah-h-h-h." It sounded like a distant cry made by someone falling off an unbelievable height.

So now he knew it hadn't been necessary to waste any words at all, except for the first few that got things started.

The skin of her arm was smooth and rich, warm under his fingers. It seemed to vibrate when he touched it. Gently, he kneaded her flesh with his fingers, then he moved his hand back and forth along her arm, stroking the glowing skin.

Slowly her head came down, jerking lower and lower until her chin almost touched her chest. He could hear her breathing plainly now. Before her head had fallen too far down, she shuddered and exhaled, "Huh!" two or three times. Her throat and head seemed to pulse, as if they responded to every beat of her heart.

Wilder decided not to waste any more time in here.

"Let's go," he suggested. His voice was getting a little thick.

She looked at him. Her mouth twisted. A shadow of pain crossed her face. Her lips were shaking when she opened them to speak. Through a soft dim cloud that had begun to veil her eyes, he could see the hot angry light coming back.

Before she could snap at him and wreck the whole pickup, he added, "We'll find another place. This one's dead."

Sliding off his stool, he waited.

She thought it over, then nodded, apparently satisfied. But when he tried to help her down from her barstool, she wouldn't let him touch her.

When they left, he held the front door for her.

Outside, the wind chilled Wilder through his clothes. He had been working up one hell of a sweat in there.

Bathed by the neon lights, she stood on the gravel, staring blindly across the highway, not seeing the cars and trucks swishing and roaring past in the night. Wilder walked off toward where he'd parked his renter, but the girl stayed where she was, so he came back.

He put a hand on her arm, near the elbow, but she jerked it out of his grasp. Peering at her unyielding profile, he was thinking, *What kind of a nut did I latch onto, here, anyway?*

She went on staring across the highway for several moments, then took a deep breath, inhaling carefully, with her mouth slightly open. "I have a car . . . with me," she said.

She almost got it out alright but her voice broke on the last two words. The cracking, scratchy sound was back and she heard it.

She looked as if she were going to cry. She sobbed once and turned her face away from him, raising one hand quickly and pressing her mouth into the palm of her hand.

Wilder pretended he hadn't noticed. "We'll use my car," he told her. "I can always bring you back here if you want yours later."

He took hold of her arm again. Her creamy, warm flesh flinched at the touch of his fingers. She pulled the arm away and turned toward him, raising her face and holding her head high once again.

She still wouldn't look at him. Impatient, Wilder watched her white angry face for a moment. Then he turned and walked around to the side of the parking lot where he had left his rented load out of reach of the neon.

The woman followed a few steps behind him.

He opened the door on her side first. He didn't bother trying to help her get in. He was getting slightly fed up with her hands-off act.

A sickle moon illuminated the night, there beyond the reach of the neon.

When the woman slid quickly inside the car, Wilder caught another glimpse of white thigh. But this time she pulled her skirt down, viciously.

Wilder slammed the door, went around, and got in on the driver's side.

Putting the key into the ignition, he glanced across at her. She sat with her hands lying flat on her little black handbag in her lap. Except her hands weren't just lying there. Enough thin moonlight shone in on her side for him to see that her hands pressed down on the bag hard.

She was hot, then cold. Angry one second, then . . .

He let go of the ignition key. For the hell of it, he reached over, laid his arm along the top of the seat, and put his hand on the back of her neck.

She jumped as if he had stabbed her. Sitting up straight, she leaned forward, trying to get away from his hand.

"Listen, you," she panted, "I don't like a fast worker . . ."

But again her voice betrayed her and came apart, cracking in the middle of the sentence. Whatever she was trying to say faltered and ended in a small high-pitched cry that was almost a whine. Gasping, she bit the sound off so abruptly that she gulped.

Ignoring her, Wilder slid his hand down the back of her neck, in under the top of her dress in back, caressing the smooth skin that seemed to radiate heat. She lurched farther forward, still trying to get clear of his hand, but he kept the hand where it was.

A grating sound began low in her throat, but it didn't come out as words, because she had her lips closed tight again.

Once more, he could hear her labored breathing — short, shuddering breaths, in and out. She opened her mouth, tried to speak again, but she couldn't seem to get the words started, just the beginning sounds — harsh, scratchy.

Her eyes closed. She looked like she was about to cry. Then her voice stopped. The last ragged sound seemed to hang there.

All at once, she slumped down in her seat. Then she leaned back, sat up straight, and opened her eyes wide.

Staring straight ahead through the windshield at the traffic whipping and growling by on the highway, she tilted her head back. Slowly, her eyes closed again and she leaned back heavily against his hand. She turned toward him. Her white face came nearer. Then she was in his arms, moaning softly into his ear, "Please be good for me. Just this once, let it be good for me."

Her lips jumped uncontrollably against his mouth. Her arms went around him. She pulled him close against her with all of her strength.

When Wilder finally tore his lips away from hers and came up for air, she panted in a small tight voice, "Oh, hurry, hurry. Can't you hurry?"

"In here?"

"Yes, yes," she whispered desperately, as if she were trying to reason with him about a completely unimportant obstacle. "Hurry, please. I beg you, please hurry. Can't you be quicker?"

"Sure," Wilder growled, "but let's get in back, okay? Damn if I want my ankles catching in the steering wheel."

Somehow he got her arms unwrapped from around him and went over the back of the seat. Then he tried to drag her over the seat top too.

"Straighten your legs, can't you?"

Her arms were around his neck again.

"Look, just for a second," he urged. "Straighten your legs."

"I can't," she whimpered. Then she almost screamed, "Oh, why can't you hurry? Why? Why?"

Her face was pressed against his. Hot tears scalded him and ran down the side of his face.

Cursing under his breath, Wilder released the grip he had on her and leaned over the seat back as far as he could with her arms still locked around his neck. Getting a grip on her legs, he bent them any way he had to, and managed to drag the rest of her over into the backseat. She landed on top of him.

When he finally got things untangled, she sank down on the backseat, still crying, her hands still reaching up for him.

"Okay, honey," he murmured. "Just one more second."

Her black skirt slid slowly away and down. White thighs seemed to gleam in the dark. He wasn't quick enough to keep them from opening, so he had to get her knees together again and hold them that way with one arm while he slid the wisp of black silk down her legs and off over her shoes.

As an afterthought, he got her shoes off too. Then he released her legs again.

When he was ready, he leaned forward above her. Her smooth, soft thighs came brushing against his naked hips, opening farther. Her hands caressed his face tenderly. Wet from crying, her face pressed against his. She kissed his face and she seemed to be singing softly in an incredibly high tiny voice. She wasn't singing words, just making soft crooning noises that sounded as if they were coming from a long way off.

Wilder couldn't make out any of it, until her lips were close to his ear, when it was starting. Softly, she murmured in this infinitesimal far-off voice, "Oh, thank you, thank you! How beautiful you are! Oh, my darling, you're so good to me, so very good to me. I'll love you always, aaaah-h-h-h! . . . thank you . . ."

Then he didn't know or care what she was saying anymore. The hot writhing volcano engulfed him.

CHAPTER TWO

Wilder took her to his motel. It might not be smart, but she was married, so they couldn't go to her place.

Anyway, she wouldn't be hanging around long. They usually had to be home before morning.

The quick one in the back seat of his rented car hadn't been enough for either of them. The second one, here in the bed, was a lot better. She did some whooping in the middle of it, and afterward she was still as jumpy as ever, but getting her rocks off helped some. Now her voice wasn't screeching and cracking so much. It sounded nicer: rich, low, and warm.

The third one was the best of all. She let him work on her awhile before he went in, so she was jolting the juice out all through that one, right from the start. It was just as well, too, because that was a shorter run than the first two. Wilder was running dry.

When it was over and they were lying there smoking, she sighed and lay snuggled against his side. Now her skin was cool.

"My name's Glorieta," she murmured. Her voice no longer had any scratching noises left in it; she was completely relaxed. It showed in her voice, soft and sweet sounding and just there, waiting for him to keep it like that.

Wilder could see why both men and women thought it was love and were always making it into such a big deal.

He was almost thinking that way now, just from listening to her, and from the way she kept kissing him and pressing herself against him under the bedsheet.

After awhile, she got out of bed, turned the lights on, and got back in beside him. She had good big breasts. When she noticed him looking at them as she was climbing up onto the bed again, she stopped and let him get a good look, smiling down at him.

He watched them swinging softly, heavily, back and forth. Reaching out, he touched her nipples with the thumbs and index fingers of both hands.

She stayed like that, on her hands and knees, while the soft happy look came back to her face and her eyes dreamed.

Then, suddenly, she plumped down, half on top of him again. He had nothing more, though, not right then, but when her exploring hand told her that, she didn't get mad.

Propping her head on her hand, she leaned her elbow in the pillow beside his head and gazed at his face.

"You're a tough one, aren't you?" she asked softly.

Wilder shrugged, but for a moment didn't reply. Then he chuckled. "Sure, baby, I'm a tiger."

She kept studying his face, tracing along the line of his jaw with a soft cool fingertip. "Your eyes look like granite," she murmured. "What's your name?"

"Dan Wilder."

That was what the papers in his wallet said. He could have gotten papers that said some other name too. After the casino grab tomorrow night, he might have to, just to be careful.

"You're not from around here, are you?"

"No."

"That's right. You wouldn't be. Or you would have known."

"Known what?"

"Oh," she sighed, "that I'm married."

Good thing you are, he thought. If he had to get it up three times a night on a regular basis . . .

Wasn't there a joke? Something about a guy getting knighted twice and complaining that once a night was enough? He forgot how it went, but he chuckled, remembering it.

"What is it?" she asked. "That I'm married?"

"No. Just an old joke I remembered."

Absently, she nodded. When she spoke, she sounded wistful. "Do you come through here often? I was thinking, maybe I could get a mailbox or something, here in Thomaston. You could write to it and tell me when you were coming through here again . . ."

"Sounds like a good idea," he said.

Who knows? he was thinking. He might even be able to take her up on it. A piece like this, anytime he wanted it, no strings . . .

The outside door burst open. Two men came charging in.

Snarling, Wilder sat up in bed. "What the hell!"

Beside him, Glorieta twisted frantically, trying to cover herself with the sheet. But when Wilder sat up suddenly, he pulled the sheet down to her waist. She kept clawing at it, but she couldn't quite cover her breasts.

"Dan, get off the sheet, will you?" she snapped irritably.

But Wilder's mind was clicking away. He hadn't heard them pick the lock. That meant the motel manager had given them a key to the room.

"Danny, will you move?" Glorieta rasped frantically.

Glancing at her, he saw what she wanted and shifted enough so she could get more of the sheet up over herself. Then he returned his attention to the two intruders. They were both grinning. The bigger one needed work done on his teeth.

"All finished?" he was asking Wilder. The smaller plump man was closing the motel unit's door. "Too bad," the big one said. "I like to catch her in the middle of a jounce. She throws a damn good hump."

Wilder flicked a quick glance at Glorieta. A badger game? No, not her. She had the sheet up to her chin and she looked boiling mad. She wasn't in on this.

"Get the hell out of here," Wilder growled. Throwing off the sheet, he rolled quickly off the bed. The bigger one brought out a revolver. Wilder stopped moving and looked from the gun to the man's face. "Alright, now what?"

"We're police."

"What's wrong?" Wilder asked. "I think she's eighteen."

The big one's grin widened, showing more of his bad teeth. "Eighteen and then some," he snickered.

The other cop told Wilder, "Relax. It's her we're after." He turned to Glorieta. "You can dress in the bathroom, Mrs. Duncan."

Glorieta didn't look at him. She went on staring up at the ceiling, her face pinched and furious. "Thanks a lot!" she snapped bitterly.

The smaller one shrugged. "Don't worry," he reassured her.

"Keep the sheet wrapped around you. We won't see anything."

The bigger one snickered again. "What'll lover-boy do, Morey? If she takes the sheet, he won't have one for himself."

Wilder looked down at himself and reached for his clothes. Behind him, he could hear her sliding out of bed.

As he snapped the fasteners on his shorts, he turned and saw her standing on her side of the bed. She kept the sheet between herself and the two plainclothes men. Wilder took one last look down the length of her body before she wrapped the sheet around herself: the broad shoulders tapering down like a wedge to her narrow waist, then spreading smooth and wide, out over the soft hips, and down the longer wedge of her thighs and calves to the ankles.

With one swift sweep of the sheet, she turned, and all of it was covered. Then she just stood there, looking like a white-faced mummy with black, snapping, angry eyes.

She stared back at Wilder with one of those fathomless, unreadable looks, as if she had never laid eyes onhim before.

He was beginning to wish she hadn't.

"Well, what about it, Mrs. Duncan?" the cop with the bad teeth asked in a harsh voice.

Without bothering to answer him, she turned and gathered up her clothes. With her bare feet slapping the floor, she padded across the room and slammed the bathroom door behind her.

Wilder went on with his dressing, his mind racing, building up a detailed story to cover his presence in this town, in case he needed one. He was about to get into his trousers when the bigger cop said, "Hold it a minute, mister."

Wilder looked over at him. "What now?"

The cop studied him a moment before telling the other one, "Morey, go through this guy's clothes. He's taking all this too much in stride."

Morey glanced at Wilder, nodded in agreement at whatever he saw in Wilder's face, and went over to search his suitcase and finger through the rest of his clothes. When that was done, he held out a hand. "The pants."

Wilder handed them over.

"Just what is this? Am I arrested?"

They ignored him. Morey searched Wilder's pants and told the other one, "No hardware." He checked Wilder's wallet.

"Name's Wilder. Sells auto batteries." He skimmed through the rest of the papers in Wilder's wallet, then said, "Seems okay."

The big cop hesitated, then nodded and put his gun away. "Alright, you. Finish your dressing. Hurry it up."

Wilder got the rest of his clothes on.

It was a good thing he hadn't seen Milo earlier in the evening, he decided. He would have gotten the gun for the casino job by now and these law would have found it on him. That would have been cute.

But then, if he had seen Milo earlier, he never would have gotten mixed up with Glorieta. Not that she wasn't a terrific bounce job, but she attracted too much attention. The wrong kind of attention.

The shorter cop was saying, "You want me to take her, Tate?"

"Not on your life!" Tate chortled. "I like to see the look on the old slob's face whenever we bring the bitch home to him after one of these outings of hers. You stay and handle this end of it. You can take her home next time."

"Okay," Morey agreed. "I'd better call them now, while you're still here." He went over to the phone and started tapping in a number.

Glorieta emerged from the bathroom fully dressed. She didn't look at any of them, just walked straight across the room to the outside door and stood beside it, facing the wall. As she passed him, Tate turned his head slowly, looking her up and down elaborately in her tight-fitting black silk outfit. He was sniffing and grinning.

Winking at Morey, he said to Glorieta's back, "Hey, Mrs. Duncan, baby, ain't you gonna wait for me? I'm your truant officer, remember? No fair sneaking off to the playground . . ."

"Let's just go," Glorieta said quietly. "Please, let's get it over with. God, I'm so sick of all of it, and of all of you . . ."

"Ain't you gonna say good-bye to lover boy Wilder?" Tate jeered. "Don't you wanna take one last look at his face, even? It won't look like that by morning, you know. None of them ever do."

She took a quick deep breath, but she still didn't turn around. She went on staring at the wall beside the door. Then she spoke deliberately. "Why should I look at him? What do I care about him? Or any of them?"

In mock reproval, Tate shook his head, smirking at Wilder, who was still standing in his shirtsleeves, taking it all in.

Over by the desk, Morey droned into the phone.

"Too bad," Tate told Wilder mockingly. "Sometimes I think Mrs. Duncan just ain't got any kind of heart. Just that other thing, further south. Well, toughie, it sure was good while it lasted, wasn't it?"

Wilder didn't reply.

Tate stared at him a moment, then turned and gazed at the woman waiting by the door with her back to the room. The smile disappeared from his wet lips. His eyes traveled hungrily down Glorieta's back and up again. His lips tightened. Going past her to the door, he opened it and followed her on out.

Morey was still on the phone. "Make it fast, will you, Riker?" he finished. "I've got to stay with this guy till your boys get out here." Hanging up, he glanced at Wilder. "Sit down, Wilder. Don't get frisky," he ordered. "No, not in that chair. Better sit in the straight one over here, where I can keep an eye on you."

Wilder sat on the edge of the straight chair against the wall beside the little desk. His legs were gathered under him while he watched Morey. "Now what?" he asked.

"Now we wait," Morey replied, teetering on his heels in the middle of the room.

"Wait for what?"

"For the boys to get out here."

"What boys?"

"Just some friends of mine." Morey grinned.

"More cops? How much law does it take to handle a shackjob in this town?"

Morey laughed. "These boys ain't cops."

"Who are they?"

Morey shrugged but didn't answer.

"What gives here, anyway? Am I under arrest?"

"Why would you be arrested? You done something we don't know about?"

"If I'm not under arrest, what's keeping you?"

"I already told you. I'm waiting for these friends."

"Then what happens?"

"Then I take off and the rest happens."

"What's the rest?"

Morey shook his head, saying plaintively, "You don't want to know that, toughie. Why not just wait and see what happens? Like a surprise."

"Your buddy Tate said something about my face won't look the same by morning."

"Ah, you don't want to pay too much attention to Tate. Old Tate does a lot of talking."

"These friends of yours," Wilder persisted. "They'd be the face-changers, is that it?"

"Well, I guess they might push you around a little. Before they start you on your way out of town."

Wilder shifted in his chair.

"Don't get up, toughie," Morey cautioned sharply. His hand slid partway inside his coat toward the gun slung under his arm. "We keep this clean and neat and friendly, okay?"

Wilder settled back onto the edge of the chair and stared at Morey's complacent cop face. "This happens to every guy who picks her up?"

Morey grinned and nodded. "That husband of hers draws a lot of water in this town."

"He must."

"We like him to be happy. If we keep an eye on his bim, he's happy."

Wilder threw back his head and laughed. "I'll bet he is. City fuzz fronting for the local tall man." Morey's eyes narrowed but he didn't say anything. "So every time little Glorieta Duncan goes out for her kicks, she's tailed. Then you two bozos bust in on the loving couple, like you did with us just now, drag her along home to hubby, and the lucky make out guy gets his head busted open by some local strong-arms. Wow, what a town!"

"They won't bust your head open, toughie," Morey protested benevolently. "Oh, they might bend it a little out of shape, but they won't bust it open. These boys are pros. They know their work."

Wilder sat there, silent, thinking about it.

Morey eyed him a moment before adding, "I told you, toughie. Remember? I said, 'You don't want to know about this.' But no, you gotta get a preview of things to come. So now you're sitting there getting all sweated up about what the boys are gonna do to you. If you didn't know, you wouldn't worry, right? Never worry about tomorrow. That's the best way to work it."

"It's not tomorrow I'm worried about," Wilder said wryly. "It's tonight."

Morey laughed. "That's good. You're alright, toughie." He laughed again. "Worried about tonight."

Wilder lunged forward, reaching back and grabbing the chair by the crosspiece atop the backrest. Morey stepped back.

"Don't do it, toughie," he yelled. "Don't try it."

His hand dove under his coat. By then, Wilder had the chair swinging through the air in an arc, out at arm's length. Morey got his service revolver out. He hollered something. Wilder didn't hear. He sent the chair sailing across the room and followed it. The chair hit Morey in the middle and knocked him backward, but he hung onto his gun.

Wilder went in low. The chair hurt Morey when it hit him. He howled and stumbled against the far wall, kicking savagely at the chair to get it out of his way.

Then Wilder was on top of him. He grabbed Morey's gun arm with both hands and drove his shoulder into Morey's ribs with his weight shoving hard behind it. Morey slammed into the wall again, banging his head against it.

Rebounding, Wilder held on tight, pulling Morey's gun arm straight out, hauling on it until Morey was pulled away from the wall, off balance, tilting to one side. Then Wilder ducked under the arm still holding onto the wrist with both hands, straightened, turned toward Morey, and twisted the arm up behind him, shoving it high.

Morey cried out in pain, and the gun fell and hit the carpet. Wilder drove Morey forward into the middle of the room, tripped him, and followed him all the way down, still keeping a tight grip on Morey's right arm twisted behind his back.

Morey's soft weight hit the floor with a sodden crash.

When he landed, Wilder released the arm. Before Morey could recover, Wilder jolted a short chop into the back of his neck. After that, Morey didn't move.

Quickly, Wilder scooped up the revolver and stuck it inside his belt. After packing his suitcase, he grabbed a hand towel in the bathroom and went over the place swiftly, erasing his fingerprints from anything he might have touched since checking in before supper.

When he was satisfied, he took the suitcase outside, wiped Morey's gun clean of prints and left it on the floor, just inside the door.

With one final swipe of the doorknobs on both sides of the door, he dropped the towel inside, picked up the suitcase, closed the door, and went out to his rented car.

He drove out onto the highway just as another car turned into the motor court. The two men in the arriving car didn't look his way as far as Wilder could see, but he didn't wait around to find out if they were Morey's friends or not. He cut south.

When he was beyond the city limit, he kept an eye peeled for a roadside phone. The first one he spotted was at the corner of a gas station.

Wilder used it with the car door open right beside it, the motor still running.

The phone rang only twice at the other end before Milo picked it up, saying, "Hello?"

"Now you answer, you bastard," Wilder snarled. "Where the hell were you all evening?"

"What? All evening? It's only eleven. Who's this?"

"Wilder. Who do you think it is?"

"You were supposed to call last night."

"I couldn't make it last night, damn it to hell."

"Okay, okay, Wilder. Don't get sore. You here in town?"

"Yeah, where else? Listen, I can't . . ."

"Come on over. 117 Locust. Where are you at? I'll give you direc—"

"Doesn't matter where I'm at, I can't make the grab. You'll have to get someone else."

"You can't make the . . . what's that supposed to mean, you can't make—"

"It means just that. I can't pull the job. Get somebody else. I'll tell you about it sometime. So long, Milo." Milo was still squawking at the other end when Wilder hung up on him.

Jumping into the car, he moved off southward, fast.

For a stretch, on both sides of the highway there were still suburban houses. After that, the road ran between modernistic plants for light industry. Off across an open stretch on his right, Wilder saw a big green neon sign that read:

DUNCAN AIRCRAFT
PLANT 2

Duncan? Was that the local wheel Glorieta was married to? One of those cops back there had called her Mrs. Duncan. And Plant Two? How big was Plant One, if that was number two?

After that one big layout, for a couple of miles there were smaller factories. Then there was nothing but farms and distant lights in houses way off.

Then there was only darkness and occasional cars coming toward Wilder through the night. Not many cars going his way were moving as fast as Wilder was, and only one car went faster. That one had a siren.

The siren wasn't turned on until it was close behind Wilder's renter. By then, he had no choice.

Slowing, he pulled over onto the shoulder of the road and sat there while the uniformed trooper came up.

"Speeding?" Wilder asked, getting out his wallet for the fake driver's license and registration papers.

"No, you weren't speeding. Your name Wilder?"

Wilder looked up into the big impassive face. Wow, what a town!

"Yes," he said disgustedly, "my name's Wilder."

CHAPTER THREE

Morey was waiting on the top step of the concrete stoop behind the municipal building.

"Good, you got the bastard," Morey exulted.

The highway patrolman had turned Wilder over to two squad car men. They led him up the steps.

"Great work, boys," Morey told them. "He give you any trouble?"

Handcuffs had been snapped onto Wilder's right wrist. The cop holding the other end of the cuffs shook his head. "No trouble, Sarge."

"That's good." Morey grinned. "Mr. Wilder will wish he didn't give me no trouble, either."

Clapping his own handcuffs on Wilder's other wrist, he told the uniformed cop, "Might as well take yours off. You'll be going right out again, anyway, after you book this bastard."

Nodding, the cop dug out a key while Morey dragged Wilder toward the doorway. An overhead lightbulb inside a wire cage projected from brickwork above the doorway. Its dim light revealed a white patch of bandage peeping from behind one of Morey's ears.

Pushing the door open, Morey hauled Wilder inside a tile floored corridor out of the light. Stopping partway along the corridor, he dug knuckles into Wilder's chest bone, stopping him too. He grinned up into Wilder's face.

"I thought maybe he'd give you boys some trouble, like he give me and Tate at the motel."

"Naw," the cop said, shaking his head again. "You want me to take my cuffs off him now, Sarge?"

"In a minute," Morey replied, reaching under his suit coat with his right hand. "First, I got to pay this punk what I owe him, for the kick in the head he handed me."

His arm swung up. Wilder tried to back away. Morey jerked the cuffs. The steel felt as if it were biting into the bones of Wilder's left wrist. He tried to reach the link chain with his fingers, but he couldn't.

Morey yanked harder on the cuffs. "Stand still, toughie," he hissed bitterly.

Wilder kept watching Morey's upraised arm. He couldn't see what Morey was holding but he knew it was bad news. All he could do was pull back and try to keep away from it.

"Stand still, I said," Morey snarled again.

Wilder had to go along: the steel felt about to break his wrist bones.

Morey's other arm swung down. Twisting away, Wilder bumped into the cop. A soft swishing sound whistled past, inches from Wilder's face.

"Hang onto your bracelets," Morey told the cop in a quiet, matter-of-fact voice. "Hold this punk steady for me."

Both of them pulled now. The two sets of handcuffs clamped to Wilder's wrists held him where he was, right between the two of them. No more side-stepping.

Morey chuckled. His teeth gleamed faintly in light from the outside bulb reflected from the corridor tiles.

Morey's arm swung up and chopped down. Wilder threw himself backward, but the cop was braced on the one arm, and Morey followed in on the other.

An explosion went off against the side of Wilder's head. He found himself on his knees. Something rotten and slimy tasting slid around inside his mouth. He spat it out. More of it collected.

High above, Morey was saying cheerfully: "Hitting people with chairs ain't polite, toughie."

Wilder knew another one was coming, but there was nothing he could do anymore.

The sap connected with his face this time. The bones seemed to bloom with an ache like soft fire. The ache spread quickly across his face, traveling along the bones, as if it were burning into their marrows.

Morey swung again, at the other side of Wilder's face this time. It went on for a long while. Each lick seemed to hurt just as badly as all the ones before.

Wilder felt as if a thick cloud was enveloping him. From outside the cloud, he could hear one of the cops saying cautiously, "Sarge, that's enough. You'll kill the guy."

Scuffing of feet on the echoing tile-floored corridor. Then Morey's voice, panting, sounding thick, "Yeah, you're right, too much is plenty. Thanks for stopping me. I would've killed the son of a bitch, sure as apples. Make him wash up before you book him. I'm the complainant, so there won't be no trouble for you two boys. I'll tell Lt. Bricken he got those lumps before he clobbered me with that damn chair in the motel."

They were dragging Wilder to his feet. He could still taste the cold slime inside his mouth, but he couldn't seem to work his mouth anymore to spit the stuff out, so it stayed there.

They hauled him along the corridor. Then there were bright lights, but different tile flooring.

Strong hands on the back of his neck thrust his head down into water. That brought him partway out of the thick cloud. A washroom. Water overflowed the sink.

"Dry yourself."

Paper towels were thrust into his hands. He couldn't see much, yet. Only light, swimming. He wiped his face with the paper towels. The swimming lights spun around, turning into a whirlpool.

"Goddamn that Morey," one of them muttered.

"Alright, mac," another one said. "Forget the towels. I said quit rubbing. Leave your face alone. It'll dry by itself."

Then the first one again, "You all right, Wilder? Hey, are you okay? You ain't gonna be sick, are you? If you are, if you're gonna throw up, this is the place for it."

Wilder tried to say "No," but it just came out a grunt. He shook his head, no. His head went on fire again.

"All right, come on then."

Some places were brightly lighted. Others had dimmer lights. But it didn't matter – Wilder couldn't see much, anyway. A gluey veil covered his eyes, a semi-transparent glue. He could sort of see through it, but he couldn't make out anything definite. It was like looking into a big fish tank through glass of different thicknesses. Everything beyond the glass was distorted, so he just went where they pushed and shoved and hauled him.

He was rolled onto his back. The cuffs were removed from his wrists.

There was still light, strong light, but he squeezed his slits of eyes closed until the goo filling them set. That shut off most of the light. There was still some, though: a montage of lights turning on and off, flashing past, this way and that, as if he were racing along all the neon lit night streets he had ever seen, going faster and faster, whirling around corners, feeling as if he were going to fall off whatever he was riding and go sailing away out of the zipping and zooming and pirouetting lights and wind up out there in the dark someplace.

Suddenly he lost his balance, or else one of the curves went on too long and he got up too much speed. He was tilting farther and farther out. Although he kept stretching his arms behind him, trying to reach something that would help him hold on and continue the ride through the dazzling skyrocketing lights, he couldn't find anything to hold onto.

Then it happened: he tilted that final little bit and fell away, and whatever vehicle he had been riding on went flashing off into the neon sparkle, and he was on his own, swinging off and up, end over end, tilting in every direction, swallowed by the night or clouds of darkness or whatever it was. Then even the speed he was moving at wasn't really speed anymore, because soon it was too dark to tell how fast he was going. Then it wasn't very long before he didn't even feel the sensation of movement, either. When that happened, it wasn't but an instant before he stopped feeling or knowing anything.

CHAPTER FOUR

When he came awake, Wilder knew morning had come from the coughing and spitting and wheezing sounds the prisoners in other cells were making.

He got one eye open. There were no windows. It might as well have been night, so he closed the eye.

Time passed. Food was brought. By then, he could see a little with the right eye.

From the sink in the corner, he got some water on his face. This time he could dry his face.

His suit coat was there, under his head as a pillow. But no belt and no shoelaces.

The cell door opened again. The belt and laces were returned. He needed new laces. After some sweating, he got them back into his shoes and tied.

Corridors. Other men, too, moving along. A bench. Waiting.

Into a courtroom. Early morning sunlight streamed beautiful dusty shafts into the big gloom through tall windows.

A skinny old goat with a bull elephant voice, a judgment day voice. Sprinkling of people at the back, watching the things in the arena.

Wilder's turn. Quick and efficient. No law's delays here. Morey testifying. Sounds of other men. Someone beside him speaking. The someone gone. Wilder looked up one-eyed at the sunlight shafts and smelled old crimes and older complacence in the chill morning air. The old dark wood paneling reeked of tired evil and the rank stench of justice.

Now he was standing in front of the nose wheezing majesty of the law.

Assault. With a weapon. Six months to a year, county prison farm.

Cold corridors again. The same cell. More waiting on his back in the bare bunk. Door clanging open. Bracelets once more on both wrists. A big barrel of blubber in khaki, a sun-reddened face, a fat smile.

Outside now. Still cool this early, but it would be a hot day.

Blubbergut said so.

Wilder's right eye could see much better. He watched the blur of morning streets go past outside the car. Then they were out of town but not on the highway Wilder knew: on a different road.

Soon, cornfields, green meadows. Brown and white cows. Everything fat and contented, like on a calendar. But people were out there, too, so it wouldn't really be contented. There would be something wrong with them, except out here it might be slower.

"Coffee? Son, you want some coffee? Last one you'll have on the outside for six months."

"No."

"Son, you want to roll with it. Hell, six months is nothin'. When I was your age, I didn't hardly notice a stretch that short atall. One time in Montana—"

"When you were my age you weren't a number—"

"Ah, hail, son, you ain't just a number . . ."

Cheerful voice going on, a boom that filled the car.

Sun climbing higher, hotter. The land stretched out fatter. The secondary road they drove along was a few feet higher than the land around. Maybe they had flash floods. Country crossroads ahead. Bar-bee-kew. Blubbergut took the ignition key, climbed out of the car. The springs rose when his weight left them.

"Black all right for you?"

He watched Blubbergut cross the gravel yard to the counter, the hearty voice still audible talking to the counterman. Not many customers. Where would they come from? Coming back with two containers. The car sagged again.

Blubbergut switched on the radio. "Let's have some music," he said. "Entertainment while we drink this mud."

One of those wake-up voices came on. Wilder flexed his hands. The bracelets clinked softly in his lap.

He still ached all over. Around the head. Shoulders too. That Morey paid back with interest.

"What's the joke, son? Let me laugh, too. I enjoy a good laugh."

"That joke of a burg back there. Duncanville. Moreyville too."

"Waal, you're right about the Duncan part. A fine old gentleman. Too bad he lived this long. A man his age does foolish things."

So does a man my age, Wilder thought. *Or any age.*

Of all the women to make a casual pass at, he had to pick one like Glorieta Duncan. Six months. Maybe a year!

"Finished yet, son? Take your time. Nice morning. Look at her out there. Gonna be a scorcher, though. You can feel it in that sun. Just a-buildin' up, that sucker. Here, let me get rid of these containers."

Car rising once more. The enormous khaki back going over to a navy gray trash barrel.

Out on the road again. A left turn at the nearby crossroad. Sun straight ahead now and getting hotter. Brings out the dirt on the windshield.

The radio voice stops, starts again, urgent sounding now, the portentous news voice: ". . . Tate's body was found beside a dirt road west of the old salt-works . . . police have reason to believe . . . prisoner now in custody on another charge . . . Daniel Wilder suspected of murdering Detective Tate . . . revenge . . . a grudge killing . . . Wilder resisted arrest earlier in the evening . . ."

Blubbergut turned his head and stared at Wilder. Staring straight ahead, Wilder listened, his jaw tight.

Dolefully, Blubbergut shook his head.

"Son," he said quietly, "you sure had one busy night."

"I couldn't have done that killing," Wilder growled. "After I left Morey on his face in that motel, it couldn't have been more than fifteen or twenty minutes before they picked me up, miles south of town."

"Well, son, it'll come out at your trial. I wonder should I take you back right now?"

"What trial? Like this morning's? That was a trial back there?"

"You'll get a fair trial, son. No, I better not. They'll send out for you, the regular way."

Wilder laughed. "A fair trial, huh? Back there in Duncanville?"

"Now, son, you don't want to—"

Wilder stomped his left heel down hard on top of the sponge-soled accelerator boot. Blubbergut groaned and took one enormous pudgy hand off the steering wheel.

"Now, son, goddamnit, you quit that. It won't do you no damn good atall."

Twisting, Wilder drove a fist deep into the man's thick red neck, below the ear.

Blubbergut gasped. His eyes popped. His near hand was reaching over to his far side, dragging a long-barrelled Colt revolver from a worn leather belt holster. The car lunged forward, faster now, weaving from side to side on the straight road.

Blubbergut couldn't pull his foot off the gas pedal. Wilder's foot stayed jammed down on top of his and wouldn't budge.

Bracing his left hand around his manacled right wrist, Wilder slugged the enormous head again higher, closer to the ear.

Blubbergut's head was knocked far over and stayed that way. A sigh escaped his lips. Grabbing the wheel with both hands, Wilder shoved it to the left.

Blubbergut was still trying to get his revolver clear of its holster. Wilder didn't try to interfere with that: he couldn't with his hands in the cuffs. He kept them on the steering wheel and he had his left shoulder jammed hard against Blubbergut's right side.

The car's speed increased, roaring on a long angle toward the left edge of the road. Another second would do it.

Finally, Blubbergut got his revolver out. He was recovering from the slugging Wilder had given him.

Wilder stayed jammed against Blubbergut, holding onto the wheel another few seconds and hoping he could restrict the big man's use of his right arm.

It didn't work out that way. Blubbergut managed to bring the barrel of the gun cracking down onto Wilder's left forearm. It hurt but luckily there wasn't much room for the swing to pick up punch.

Wilder's left arm went dead but he kept the other hand on the wheel. The car reached the edge of the road. Now it was on the dirt shoulder. Wilder could hear the left front tire going *blup blup blup.*

Then the whole works tilted abruptly to the left and they were slithering down the short embankment, raising dry dust in a thick whirling cloud.

The steering wheel wrenched itself out of Wilder's grip.

Horrified, Blubbergut was staring, shouting, "Son, you'll kill the both of us . . ."

The car hit the bottom of the short slope below the edge of the road, hit hard, and went over on its side with a grinding sliding crash and kept going, plowing into a cornfield.

Wilder was thrown forward against the dashboard. Gritting his teeth, he kept telling himself, *Watch the head. Protect the head. There's no recovery time. Snap out of it, quick!*

Dust filled the car.

After slithering a long devastating way into the corn, the car finally came to a stop, lying on its side.

Sudden silence surrounded them. The dust began to settle, still whirling in the morning sunlight.

Wilder ended up on top of Blubbergut. And there was the gun, hanging limply from the huge pudgy hand. No motion in it.

Wilder grabbed for the gun with both his linked hands, got his knees beneath him and dug them down into the thick khaki forearm.

The gun tore loose. Then he relaxed.

He sneezed in the dust-filled car.

The revolver was a Trooper Colt, one of the .357 Magnums.

Wilder was surprised an old-timer like Blubbergut would carry anything but one of the real old frontier models. He had seemed that type.

Opening his eyes, Blubbergut stared around a moment and sighed.

"Son," he murmured, "when you make a move, you sure move wild and sudden-like . . ."

"The keys," Wilder demanded. "For these lousy bracelets."

"Sure, son, you can have the keys. Doesn't make that much of a difference. You end up in jail tomorrow morning, 'stead of today. Just take it easy. Here's your keys."

Digging them out of his shirt pocket with his left hand, the one Wilder wasn't kneeling on, he asked, "You want me to open them?"

"No, thanks, Tex," Wilder laughed. "I'll open them. You just rest there."

"Glad to rest a spell, son. I'm in pretty fair shape, for a man my age, but I never did like any kind of automobile accident. Shakes me up too much inside. The ticker feels it most. Whoowee!" he murmured with wonder glistening in his pale blue eyes. "Listen at that ole thing a-bumping away in there." Chuckling, he shook his head, listening to his heartbeat.

Swiftly, Wilder used the key and got the cuffs off. He was about to flip them away when he looked at them thoughtfully, and then shoved them into his coat pocket along with the key.

"Never know when I might need some handcuffs," he told Blubbergut.

Reaching up, he opened the car door on his side, the side now facing the sky.

"Better turn off that ignition," he advised the big man. "This thing's liable to catch fire on you."

Hastily, Blubbergut reached out and turned the ignition key. "That's right, son. I clean forgot. But you ain't gonna take them bracelets, are you? Son, I just bought that pair new last month. I need 'em in my job . . ."

Wilder put one foot on the steering post and the other on Blubbergut's right shoulder to get himself high enough so he could push the car door upward. He held it open that way for the second it took him to jump up and worm his way through the opening.

Sitting up there, he grinned down at Blubbergut, who was just beginning to struggle, trying to get himself unjammed from between the steering wheel and the seatback.

"Serves you right," Wilder told him. "It'll teach you not to go putting handcuffs on strangers."

Blubbergut still looked distressed but he chuckled. "Son, I surely wish you'd leave them bracelets here. They set me back a pretty penny."

"No," Wilder said. "I might need them. And the gun too. You can tell anyone who's interested that someday I'll be coming back up here to Thomaston, and when I do, I'll rip the goddamn dump up the middle so deep it'll need a zipper to close itself up again."

On hearing Wilder's words, Blubbergut shook his head unhappily. He started to say something but Wilder didn't listen. He'd given Blubbergut the message. Maybe for awhile they'd think he was going to head south, trying to put distance between himself and Thomaston.

That's what he wanted them to think, because he was planning on going the other way, right back up into the city.

Swinging his legs clear and still holding the car door propped up and open, he pushed himself free and dropped to the ground.

Above him, the car door dropped solidly shut. Grinning at the underpart machinery of the vehicle lying on its side, he turned and walked into the tall corn, heading away from the road toward the northwest so he would eventually cut across the secondary road they had driven down on from the city.

CHAPTER FIVE

Wilder heard the first sirens around an hour later. They came howling down from the north, somewhere ahead and to his left. From their sound, he was closer to the secondary road than he'd thought.

He dropped to the ground between rows of corn. At the dim end of a green row, dark blurs whipped past and were soon gone. The siren sounds went wailing off to the south and the crossroad "bar-bee-kew."

Up on his feet, Wilder headed straight for the road. It was slow walking in the soft earth.

The corn stood a foot taller than his head, but he moved bent over so he wouldn't rustle the tops more than he absolutely had to. They swayed gently in the breeze which didn't reach down to where Wilder was, but whenever he pushed any cornstalks aside, their tops would whip and thrash around in the hot morning silence, making him cringe and remain motionless where he stood until they settled down and were silent again.

If cops were being dropped off along the road at intervals and one or two of them were nearby, they couldn't miss spotting the disturbance Wilder kept making as he moved down the aisle between the growing corn.

He stopped where the corn ended, twenty feet from the edge of the road. Off to his right, an open pipe end big enough for a man to crawl into stuck out of the sloping ground below the road.

Remaining where he was, he tried to decide whether to get closer to the road or to stay back in the cornfield and work his way northward.

He decided against that option. The sooner he got out of the cornfield, the better. He had a feeling about it, an instinct that told him if he remained in the corn, he would be that much easier to surround and hunt down.

He tried to remember what was on the other side of the road, but he couldn't: he hadn't been paying attention on the drive down from the city in Blubbergut's car.

Alright, the best thing was to climb up the incline far enough to see across the road and find out what was over there.

He listened for the sound of approaching cars, but he couldn't hear anything except the click and hum of nearby insects buzzing about, and the soft ever present clashing corn stirred by the gentle breeze. He tried to blot the nearby sounds from his hearing and listen beyond them.

When he was reasonably certain no cars were approaching, he left the dry rustling corn and moved forward to the bottom of the slope beside the road. Leaning his weight on his fingertips, he crouched and started up the steep slope.

He was halfway up to the edge of the composition pavement when a shrieking noise seemed to start from complete silence and build with incredible swiftness into a terrifying scream. Another siren!

Wilder froze, flattening against the slope for a moment before making himself raise his head slightly to chance a quick look up at the road. He caught a glimpse of a motorcycle cop's helmeted head rushing along toward him.

Ducking, he froze for a moment, and then began scuttling backward down the slope, crawling frantically toward the big pipe nearby trying to keep low; the cop was keeping to the middle of the road and might be able to spot him in the ditch when he roared by.

Wilder made it to the pipe but he didn't have time to crawl into it. Staccato thunder split the midmorning quiet. The motorcycle cop loomed high above where he crouched trying for concealment below the big drainage pipe.

Wilder couldn't believe the cop didn't see him. His right hand slid under his suit coat in back for the six-inch-barreled Trooper Colt he had stuck under his belt.

Holding the gun, he waited. The bike jockey had nothing to do with any of this, but he was the one who would catch the first slug from this cannon.

The rattling blast of the motorcycle's cutout made Wilder clench his teeth. He squinted carefully upward, watched the trooper flash by and go on, and saw the torso and helmeted head drop lower the farther away he went until he was gone.

Incredulously, Wilder remained in his crouch a long moment until he finally realized that the cop hadn't spotted him.

Head first, he squirmed into the big open ended pipe, hurrying because more patrol cars and bike cops might be coming behind that one. For one of them to miss seeing him was a lucky break, but if he remained exposed out there . . .

Wilder knew some of the others were bound to notice him. Right now, this pipe was his best bet for concealment. He wormed his way into it.

He didn't like this. It was too dark in here but he had no choice.

It surprised him that no light was visible ahead of him at the far end across the road. The middle must be choked up with dirt.

Unless it wasn't a drainage pipe at all! Maybe it didn't extend under the road with both ends open, as he'd assumed.

Dirt and pebbles scraped beneath his chest as he crawled along.

He still hadn't gotten into the thing far enough. His feet still stuck out. He had to get farther in.

He squirmed forward another foot or two. His shoulders were too big. If he kept at this, he was going to get stuck for sure.

A trace of claustrophobia swept through him.

Cursing himself, Wilder worked his way a little farther forward, thinking that by now his feet ought to be well inside the end of the pipe behind him. To test it, he swung his lower legs upward. His heels hit the top of the pipe, so they were inside and he could relax.

Overhead he could hear cars passing. Their tires made a kind of muted thunder as they drove by. Then motorcycles came.

Wilder felt as if he were inside a drum and someone was shooting pellets against the outside of it. Long after the last of the vehicles were gone, his ears rang from the reverberations of their passing.

Something stirred in the pipe ahead. The tiny sound startled Wilder. Some kind of varmint?

Sweat poured from him. He gripped the butt of the gun he held thrust out ahead of him, but he didn't want to use it. Not in here. The echo of a shot inside this pipe might carry for miles.

Relax, he kept telling himself. What kind of critter could be in here? Whatever it was, it had to be tiny. Cut the panic.

All the same, he began crawling backward, trying not to think how small a hydrophobic skunk might be. It seemed to take a lot longer to work his way back out of the pipe than it had taken him to get in.

When his dangling, down-reaching feet made contact with the ground outside, he pulled his head and shoulders clear.

It was good to feel the sunlight and the cool feeling air again.

Swiping at the sweat almost blinding his eyes, he swung around the end of the pipe and lunged up the slope to the side of the road.

He had to get squared away before any more law came charging down on him. Flat on his chest at the roadside, he squinted both ways along it, north and south.

Heat waves shimmered above the composition. He couldn't see anything definite through them, in either direction.

On the other side of the road he could see nothing, just the far edge of the roadside. Farther off, a wide field stretched away, occasional clumps of trees, a white house, and barn.

Even if the concealment on the other side of the road wasn't as good as the cornfield behind him, Wilder decided to get over there. If he had to, he could always come back.

Hurriedly, he crawled across the rock-hard paving and slithered down the far slope, where he crouched and listened. No cars or cycles were coming.

Getting to his feet near the bottom, he spied the other end of the pipe and hunkered down beside it. Good to know he could always crawl into this end of the thing if more of his pursuers passed along the road above him.

The field to the west was mostly grass, or maybe hay, stretching off flat and wide. Partway across, it had been plowed under. Beyond the line where the plowing had been done, a long stretch of dark dirt showed. Beyond the plowed part, maybe half a mile away, the green began again; a lighter green than the nearby grass.

The only thing that moved in all that flatness was a spot of red, off to the south. The only sound except humming insects nearby was the lazy distant chug of the red tractor's motor as it worked its way on back up this way, plowing its several long straight parallel rows, turning the grass under.

* * *

No police cars or motorcycle cops were passing along the nearby road when Wilder rose from the ground beside the moving tractor and swung aboard on the side away from the road. He hunkered on his heels on a short running board beside where the tractor's driver sat perched under an umbrella.

"Keep going," Wilder said quietly, showing the Trooper Colt to the leather brown elderly man under the yellow and blue umbrella mounted behind the driver's seat.

The man's clear blue eyes widened. "Hey, you're the fella all those cops are—"

"Probably," Wilder interrupted. "Just keep this thing moving, mister."

The blue eyes studied the gun carefully. Wrinkles appeared in the brown skin around his eyes.

"That Les Perkins's pistol you got there?"

"If that's Blubbergut's name, it is," Wilder replied. "Can't you get more speed out of this Sherman tank?"

"Not much more," the farmer chuckled. "You don't want any more speed. One of them might notice."

He tilted his head over his right shoulder, eastward toward the road. "They know how fast plowing should be done. Or how slow."

"Yeah, I guess so," Wilder had to agree.

They rolled along in silence awhile, the driver high up on his seat in the shade of the beach umbrella, and Wilder precariously clinging to the short side running board beside the loud smelly tractor engine, fully exposed to the noon sun.

"You kilt that city detective, did you?" the man asked presently, not looking down at Wilder.

"No, I didn't."

The man nodded slightly and after a while of silence he shrugged almost imperceptibly. They went along like that until a voice hailed the tractor driver from the road.

"Who's that?" Wilder muttered.

"Friend of mine. State Highway Patrol," he replied, his lips barely moving.

"Use your head," Wilder said evenly.

"I'll do that."

He hollered a greeting to the man on the road.

Wilder couldn't hear what the patrolman called, but the tractor-man replied, "Okay, I'll stop off to the house and pick it up. I'd a thought you boys would've caught that feller by now."

"Not yet, but we'll have him before supper."

Wilder's mouth tightened when he heard that. There was no more yelling back and forth. The tractor continued on its way. It still wasn't moving fast, but Wilder knew it was eating up distance between himself and Thomaston's city limits, and that's all he wanted.

"What was he telling you back there?" Wilder asked. "I couldn't catch all of it."

"Tole me to pick up my carbine when I passed the house. In case you slipped past them and doubled back, up this way. They don't think you did, though."

"You don't need the carbine," Wilder told him. "This is gun enough for both of us."

Smiling slightly, the driver nodded. "It sure enough is." Then the smile went away. "You fixing to kill me?"

"No. Not if you stay sensible."

The man thought about that and nodded once more. They drove on.

Wilder left the man and the tractor in the shade of some trees about three farms north. He used the man's bootlaces to tie his hands and feet and left him out of the sun, as comfortable as a tied man can be.

The flat land went on.

Taking a chance, Wilder kept walking through the various farms he came to. Off to the northeast and northwest, he could see dim lines of hills, but nearby everything was nothing but flat. Straight ahead appeared the half-dozen or so skyscrapers Thomaston had grown for its ego. They didn't get nearer quickly, but they did get nearer.

Wilder was accosted by no one on any of the farms.

Once he saw three or four horses near the far end of a meadow he was crossing, but they didn't come near him.

A small herd of grass munching cows milled around and mooed while he walked by, too close to suit them, but those were the only other animals he saw.

Then the farms were behind him. He skirted a graveyard for rusty cars. Beyond that were weed grown railroad tracks. He came up behind a filling station and Wilder stopped back among the weeds and brush.

Removing his suit coat, he examined the front of his shirt. It was filthy. He took it off and threw it away.

The T-shirt underneath wasn't too clean and it showed some blood spots from the sapping he had gotten from Morey the night before, but the back of the T-shirt wasn't too messed up. Peeling it off, he turned it inside out and put it on again with the back of the T-shirt in front. Its neck tucked up pretty snug against his Adam's apple, but not enough to bother him after a couple of tugs loosened it some.

Pounding as much dust as he could from his coat and pants, he put the coat back on and left it unbuttoned in front because he had the barrel of the Trooper Colt stuck under his belt in back with the butt resting against his right hip bone. By leaving the coat unbuttoned, it draped loosely over the gun-bulge in back — that way the gun didn't show.

He approached the rear of the gas station on the side with a men's room sign above an outside door.

Trying the door, he found it unlocked and slipped inside. Seeing what he looked like surprised him. It was the first glimpse he had gotten of himself since Morey had worked him over the night before.

Now, underneath the sweat-streaked layers of dust he had picked up in the cornfield and inside the drainage pipe, and later the turned-over earth of the plowed field, he could see the mess Morey had made of his face.

The left eye had a full shiner. He could see out of it a little, but not much. The right eye wasn't that bad, just a bit puffed and red near the outside corner, and streaked blue underneath.

The rest of his face was lumpy and beat-up looking, here and there, from some under the skin damage Morey's sap had caused.

There weren't too many open cuts, but one was too many.

Shaking his head, he cursed Morey absently.

Turning on the faucet, he filled the little enamel sink with water and began carefully washing around his eyes.

Then he washed the rest of his face and his neck. When he was through, he didn't look quite as bad as he had before.

Drying off, he was careful with the paper towels. He didn't want to open any cuts that were healing.

When he was dry, he worked on his hair with a pocket comb.

Slipping into the suit coat, he gave himself a final inspection in the mirror and decided he could chance going into town looking like this, instead of waiting till dark. He might just be able to get through town to Milo's place, provided he kept to back streets and stayed off the highway, and had plenty of luck going for him. He was due for a supply of luck about now. Overdue.

Leaving the men's room, he went along to the front of the service station. An attendant in a clean blue jumper was filling a customer's gas tank.

Wilder strolled straight out to the road, crossed it to get under the trees on the far side, and didn't look back at the attendant and his customer. Maybe they had noticed him, maybe not.

Walking westward to the nearest corner, he turned right and was walking along on sidewalks in a quiet early afternoon neighborhood.

A few blocks ahead, a kid with schoolbooks poked along, turned a corner and was gone.

In general, Wilder adopted a zigzag route, first a couple of blocks northward, then a couple westward, trying to work his way closer to the big north-south highway.

He knew he couldn't go back to the motel where he had gotten the room the night before. The fuzz would have that staked out first thing. And the motel manager would know him. He might also know Morey and the dead one, Tate.

No point going there. The law would have taken his luggage and the rented car, and he knew they had his wallet.

The luggage wouldn't tell them a thing and the only thing Wilder could have used from the wallet was the money. The papers it held didn't mean a thing to him, not anymore, not in a squeeze this tight. Whenever he got out of this hell-town, if he got out, he'd have to collect another set of papers with a brand new name.

Murder One!

The big tag, the killing tag, and who was going to argue them out of it? A fast check on his past from the cards and things would tell them there wasn't any past. They would love that.

They'd take a second look at him, a hell of a lot closer look this time, and they'd smile and rub their mitts together with anticipation. After that, they'd have a ball, all of them: the lawyers, the judge, the witnesses, and finally the hangman, or the gas pipe guy, or however they executed them here.

Right now, it was money he needed most. That meant Milo.

What was that address Milo had told him on the phone?

Locust Street. What number, though? One seventy? No, it was lower. One seventeen.

But where in hell was Locust Street?

Who do you ask? Who do you walk up to with a face in the shape his was in and ask where anything is, without erupting a sudden panic to liven up the afternoon?

He made one of his westward jags. Four or five blocks ahead, gleaming traffic moved both ways. That would be the big highway.

He decided to get near it but not to go on it. So, two blocks along, he turned north again. Two blocks of that and he went west again.

Ahead was a barbershop. Ask there? He glanced in as he strolled by.

No, the barber was working on a customer.

A corner bar. Not there, either. Bartenders and regulars examine all non-regulars too closely.

Another northward turn for a couple of blocks, then west again. The highway was close ahead.

A candy store/grocery. An old lady inside. Wilder turned in. "Where's Locust Street, ma'am?"

It seemed to take three real long minutes, though probably it wasn't anywhere near that long. She peered toward him from the back of the store, but Wilder stayed in the street doorway with the afternoon sunlight behind him.

She knew where Locust Street was, or said she did. Pretty far downtown. Take the bus on the highway, number four bus.

"Thanks."

Wilder left the store. He didn't have bus fare, so it had to be on foot.

A radio or TV set was going somewhere. The announcer's voice broke in as soon as an ad ended.

"Police are convinced Wilder won't try to reach the city . . . roadblocks have been set up . . . all roads south of a line . . ."

The grave doomsday voice faded behind him and was gone into the afternoon silence.

Wilder grinned. They had actually gone along on that business he had fed Blubbergut. But they wouldn't go on believing it for long, not after they found the tractor driver.

He strode on, keeping his stride down to a steady, seemingly unhurried pace; that of a man who was going somewhere and was going to get there without wasting time, but who wasn't in all that much of a hurry, not so much that a cop would be likely to stop him and give him a once-over.

Unless, of course, the cop happened to see the shape his face was in.

CHAPTER SIX

One seventeen Locust Street was about fifty feet from an intersection that had a neighborhood bar on one corner, a small funeral parlor on another, an empty lot on a third, and another empty lot with a billboard on the last.

The billboard contained a movie ad showing a standing man and woman dry humping. The words claimed the picture was almost too raw to be shown on a movie screen.

Wilder got off the street as quickly as he could.

One seventeen was a glass paned door, one step up from the sidewalk. The door opened into a tiny vestibule with only one mailbox, Milo's. This was the other end of the building that held the corner bar.

A flight of brown wooden steps climbed between tan walls to a landing about fifteen feet long. At the far end of the landing was a wooden door, locked.

After trying the doorknob, Wilder looked for a buzzer button, couldn't find one, and knocked.

No one answered. Wilder listened. He couldn't hear anything. He knocked again, harder.

Still no response from beyond the door. But Wilder stayed where he was. Something told him Milo was inside.

Keeping it low, he growled, "Open up, Milo."

Still nothing.

"Open up, Milo," he said again, still keeping his voice down.

"I'm getting in there if I have to tear this goddamn door off its hinges. Open up."

Still not a whisper of sound from beyond the door.

Taking out the Trooper, he tapped the muzzle against the door panel several times.

"Milo, this is a gun. First, I shoot the lock off. Maybe anyone who hears the shot will think it's a car backfiring. Or maybe they won't . . ."

The lock turned. The door opened a crack. Close to the narrow opening, Milo's voice whispered, "Wilder, don't do this to me. Man, don't drag me into a killing. What'd I ever do to you?"

Wilder stiff-armed the door and followed it in, shoving hard against Milo's weight, sending him staggering back into the apartment. Milo tripped on the edge of a threadbare carpet and fell.

Wilder closed the landing door behind him.

Milo sat on the floor, staring up at Wilder with frightened eyes. One hand rubbed his face where the door had banged against it.

Shaking his head from side to side, he moaned, "Wilder don't drag me into it, not into a killing. I never done nothing to you, Wilder, you know I never did—"

"Shut up," Wilder said wearily. "No one saw me. The streets out there are dead this time of day. I walked all through this town and I didn't see ten people all the way, and most of those were housewives hanging over back fences."

Milo stayed on the floor and went on with his moaning.

Impatiently, Wilder told him, "Milo, shut the hell up. Get up from there. I'm here till dark. I need a shower and a briefing on this goddamn burg. And food. Lots of food."

Milo quit moaning, but he remained where he was, no longer looking up at Wilder, but staring forlornly at the floor, shaking his head.

For a moment, Wilder watched him, then stepped over to him, bent above him, and cocked a fist close under Milo's face.

Convulsively, Milo threw himself backward. "Don't hit me, Wilder," he cried.

"Lower your voice, you fool," Wilder hissed. "Go gutless on me and raise a hooraw, and I'll finish you off right now, so help me. You hear, Milo?"

Milo hesitated, then bobbed his head up and down. "Yeah," he gasped, "but don't hit me, Wilder, just please don't hit me. I can't stand it when I get hit. I just can't—"

"Shut your mouth," Wilder snarled. "Turn off this babbling, will you? Anyone would think you never saw trouble before."

Milo almost sobbed. "Man, I've seen plenty trouble, but this . . . this is a murder. They'll nail you down for this one, Wilder. Why'd you have to do it? A cop! Are you crazy? We had a sweet little grab all set for tonight. Then you have to take and cut loose. You put holes in a cop's back—"

"Milo, if I was going to put holes in anybody, do you see me doing it so they can turn me up for it? Think a minute, blockhead. I didn't pull that hit. They're hanging it on my tail because I'm handy for it, that's all."

Milo's mouth fell open. He thought about it, his eyes narrowing to help him think.

"Didn't do it?" he murmured, confused. Then his eyes blazed again with the return of his panic. "Wilder, it's been on TV all day long. They wouldn't say you did it on TV if they weren't sure—"

"They'd say the earth was flat if it jumped their ratings," Wilder jeered. Then he shrugged, impatient with himself for trying to reason with Milo.

Putting the Trooper out of sight, he grabbed Milo by the throat with both hands and hauled him to his feet. When he was sure Milo was standing, he took his hands away.

"Listen, Milo, I'll tell it to you once more: turn off the talk. Turn it off and keep it turned off. I want food and information out of you. No advice. No whining. Now get busy. Where's the kitchen?"

Milo stepped back a pace, still hesitant, watching Wilder fearfully for another moment before he turned and led the way to the kitchen at the back part of the flat.

"There ain't too much food," he said apologetically. "I don't usually stock up until—"

"Anything is a lot, the shape I'm in," Wilder interrupted. "Get it out. Save the talk to answer questions. And settle down."

Milo got busy digging food out of the refrigerator. Once he had something to do with his hands, putting food on the kitchen table, Milo began to quiet down.

Wilder went into the bathroom at the back end of the apartment beyond the kitchen. The shower didn't work, so he started water going in the tub.

Returning to the big combination bedroom/living room, he rifled a dresser for one of Milo's shirts. Shucking his suit coat, he tried to get into the shirt. It was too small. He'd have to rip it up the back and maybe slit the sleeves from the elbows up past the shoulders, then maybe it would fit. With his coat on over it, the slits wouldn't show.

Dropping the shirt and his suit coat on the sofa, he went into the kitchen. Taking two slices of bread, he put some ham and boloney and liverwurst between them and quickly ate the sandwich, washing it down with milk from a container.

When that was finished, he looked over the display of food Milo had spread out on the table and said, "Cook that steak."

Milo nodded. Reluctantly, he reached for the steak.

Wilder almost grinned. He was eating Milo's special meal.

"I'll be cleaning off some of this dirt I've picked up," he told Milo. "By the time the steak is ready, I should be through in there. And Milo . . . don't try a bugout. And stay away from the phone."

Milo didn't look at him. Wilder watched him a moment.

"Understand?"

Milo nodded.

Wilder went into the bathroom. The water was too hot, so he added cold and got his clothes off. Filling the sink with water, he dropped his underwear and socks into it and a small sliver of soap with them.

By then, the water in the tub was ready, so he turned the faucets off and got in, laying the Trooper on a little three-legged stool with a plastic covered seat within easy reach. Sinking into the water, Wilder just lay there awhile, giving it time to work on him and relax his muscles.

Milo was one of those victims of an adolescent stickup attempt who had gotten caught, and was just old enough at the time to get put behind the walls. When they let him out, he was never good for anything again, like most. That was the way the system worked it.

Milo had no guts left, so he couldn't handle anything but the harmless rackets. Getting regular work was out because of his criminal record, which always made a difference no matter what they claimed about rehabilitation.

So Milo was hung up for life, dangling in nowhere land among an ocean of other slobs just like himself hanging around bus terminals, cruddy bars, cheap whorehouses, filling in sometimes with a shadow job or a brainwashing detail for one of the big private dick outfits, making pin money the best way he could, anyway he could.

While Wilder was scrubbing the grime off, he thought about Milo.

He knew Milo couldn't be trusted in anything dangerous. Most people were the same: they couldn't be trusted either, so that was nothing particular against Milo. But in this present emergency, Wilder had to make sure he didn't let his own vital needs delude him into depending on someone like Milo any more than he had to. There might be last desperate helping hands you could grab hold of in this world, to keep it from grinding you under, but Milo's hand wasn't one of them.

Getting out of the tub, Wilder started draining the water.

Grabbing a big towel, he stepped, dripping, out of the bathroom to see what Milo was up to in the kitchen. Steak frying smells filled the little room. Milo glanced up at him dripping in the doorway, then looked sullenly back down at the frying pan again.

Returning to the bathroom, Wilder finished drying himself and spent five careful minutes shaving gingerly around the cuts and lumps and sore spots on his face. The left eye hadn't improved any, and it probably wouldn't for days, maybe weeks. The right one didn't look too bad. The razor opened up some of the cuts, but Wilder knew his blood clotted quickly, so he just dried his face and didn't bother with any medication.

Giving the socks and underwear a fast scrub in the sink with the sliver of soap, he wrung them out and hung them up to dry on the high shower curtain rail across from the open bathroom window. The breeze would speed the drying process.

Climbing into his trousers, he went back out to the kitchen.

Milo had the steak cooked and ready. Wilder ate it, with Milo seated across the table, watching. When the steak was down, Wilder ate a dish of leftover cold peas, had Milo warm a small can of beans, ate a stalk of celery, drank some orange soda, some more milk, and ended the meal with two cups of coffee, also left over from that morning.

Smoking with his coffee, Wilder leaned back. "Where's that cop Morey live?"

Milo shook his head. "Offhand, I don't know. You want me to see if he's in the phone book?"

"Yeah, good idea."

Milo got up and left the kitchen.

"Bring the phone book in here," Wilder called after him. The gun he had stuck into his belt in back made his skin itch, so Wilder took it out and laid it on the table next to his coffee cup.

Milo brought in the phone book, stopped short at the sight of the gun on the table, then came hesitantly in the rest of the way, with the phone book open, pretending he hadn't seen the gun. He cleared his throat as he seated himself again across from Wilder and said, "Yeah, this is probably him."

He turned the book around and held it out toward Wilder, pointing a finger at Morey's name and address on the page.

Wilder read the address. "You got a map of this town?"

"I think so. I used to have one."

"See if you can find it."

Milo started out of the kitchen, carrying the phone book with him. "Leave the book here," Wilder told him.

Taking the book from Milo, he read Morey's address again to make sure he had it right. He could hear Milo pulling out dresser drawers in the big room.

While he was waiting, Wilder looked up the name Duncan.

There were about fifteen of them. He didn't know which of the listed Duncans was the one he wanted.

He called in to Milo, "The Duncan who throws all the weight around, what's his first name?"

Milo appeared in the kitchen doorway with a street map. "What?"

"You know of a big operator around here named Duncan?"

"Sure. What do you want with him?"

"Never mind what I want with him. What's his name?"

Milo stared at him. "Duncan."

"His first name, for Christ's sake."

"Oh. Jeff. Jeff Duncan. He's an old man . . ."

Wilder ignored the rest. He delved into the book again.

"There's no Jeff Duncan listed here."

Milo thought a minute and nodded. "Maybe he's only got unlisted numbers," he suggested.

Wilder grimaced. "Yeah, that's probably it. Where does he live?"

"How should I know where he lives, Wilder? Off in Breaker Hills, where the rest of the rich ones live."

"So where's Breaker Hills?"

Milo turned and pointed out the kitchen window behind Wilder. Turning in his chair, Wilder saw the green line of hills northwest of the city.

Well, it wasn't pinpointing anything for him, so he'd have to find out Duncan's address some other way. Maybe Morey would tell him once he got his hands on the bastard.

"Fill me in on this Duncan," he told Milo.

"Well, I don't know too much about him. He's rich. He's old now, like I said, but he still runs things, mostly through Bert Hendricks."

"Who's Hendricks?"

"He's the guy you have to see if you want anything. You know, the operator, the in-type. Politics, the vote, the rackets. Steer clear of him, Wilder. His people are bad medicine. This is their town. They run things, all around here."

Grimly, Wilder nodded. "Ahuh," he agreed. "Somebody runs things, that's for sure." He stared at the phone book in front of him until a grin touched his lips.

"So it's their town, is it? Well, maybe I'll take it away from them for awhile. Maybe I'll even take it away from them for good. Or them away from it, anyway." With an angry expression on his face, he stared across the nearby rooftops at the distant line of hills, Breaker Hills. "Yeah," he murmured, grinning wolfishly. "I might just do that."

Facing Milo again, he caught a look of bewilderment and apprehension on his face, and laughed at the sight.

"Okay, Milo, before you close your mouth, what about Duncan? I get the picture. He runs things around here. Anything more?"

"Well, like I told you, he's old. Now Hendricks does the actual work, handles the details. That's the way it worked out, I guess. There was a couple of other guys, a few years back, but they . . . well, I guess they went away."

Wilder laughed. "I guess. Go on."

"This Hendricks is a lawyer. He . . . operates."

Milo tried to find other words but he couldn't. He ended up spreading his hands and shrugging. He couldn't say it any better than he already had.

Wilder knew what he meant, though. He also knew by now that anything he learned from Milo he was going to have to dig out of him patiently. He tried to be patient.

"What about the place you fingered for me?" Wilder asked.

"That gambling joint we were supposed to knock over tonight? Is that one of this Hendricks's operations?"

"Sure," Milo replied, on firm ground again. "Oh, I don't mean he owns it, but if he didn't want it running, it wouldn't stay open."

"And if Jeff Duncan got over being old tomorrow and wanted it burnt down, this Hendricks would burn it down?"

"Somebody would burn it down." Milo grinned but he was looking uneasy again. "You're not going to burn it down, are you, Wilder?"

Wilder laughed. "Hell no," he said. After thinking it over until he was satisfied, Wilder nodded.

"Good enough. Duncan, then Hendricks."

He copied Hendricks's address and phone number from the book.

"But first, Morey. You know anything about Morey I can use?"

"Well . . . he's a cop."

Wilder sighed. "I know he's a cop. What about him?"

Milo was getting spooked again.

Wilder watched him a second and then said softly, "Milo, don't go dumb on me, okay? Morey's the one that's been driving this bum peg into my back. What about him? I know he's not straight, but how crooked is he?"

Milo licked his lips. "Well, he's in with some of Hendricks's operations. Him and Tate. Or Tate was, before he . . . Morey lives in a pretty swell neighborhood. I mean, swell for a cop."

"Figures. You got a newspaper? I can use a little more dope about how I killed Tate last night, while I was getting dragged back into town by that highway patrolman. I'm better than I thought I was."

"No papers," Milo said. "But they been showing it on TV all day."

"Turn on the TV, then," Wilder said, following him out to the big room.

Wilder sat on the sofa and watched the television. Some kind of soap opera was showing, not news.

"Try another station."

"This is the best one for news coverage," Milo said carefully, moving his hand tentatively toward the remote to change stations if Wilder insisted. "This show they got on is over at 4:30. Then they have news again."

"Alright, leave it on," Wilder said, getting up and going into the bathroom to see if his socks and underwear were dry yet. Everything was still damp.

Back on the sofa, he watched the big TV faces and the eyes and the pores of their skin and listened to them hollering and crying about whatever it was that was breaking their hearts.

It was worse than the old B-movies used to be, but he had heard somewhere that the companies who advertised paid out heavy sugar, which would explain why the actors did this kind of crud.

At 4:30 the news came on. It showed a lot of patrol cars and motorcycles swirling dust, and square-jawed law out in the hot afternoon sun. The commentator on the spot was sticking his mike into faces now and then, and getting dumb answers to his dumb questions, but not much else.

They showed Blubbergut's overturned car and the announcer gave a quick rundown of the story from the beginning. The only thing that interested Wilder was that they hadn't found Tate's body until early in the morning, which meant they didn't know when he'd been shot, just sometime last night.

So they could put any time they felt like on the killing.

Apparently, they felt like putting a time on it that would fit Wilder's time frame. It might be a tight fit, but Wilder knew he was the only one who would do any complaining about it.

Then there was a shot of Morey giving an indoor interview, probably from a newscast earlier in the day.

Morey gave the usual meticulous cop's report, except he claimed Tate had still been in the motel room when Wilder had started to swing the chair and put Morey out of action.

The implication Morey's testimony made was unmistakable. Wilder would have been the last one to see Tate alive. There was no mention of Glorieta Duncan. Wilder wasn't at all surprised.

When the world news came on, he lost interest. "Okay, Milo, turn it off."

More to himself than to Milo, he mused aloud, "I wonder who really did kill that Tate bastard?"

Milo used the remote to switch off the screen and crossed the room gingerly to sit on the edge of an armchair near the window.

Milo was nervous again. He kept watching Wilder, who stared back at him fixedly, but he wasn't seeing Milo: he was thinking.

"They're covering for her, that's basic," Wilder murmured after awhile. "Somehow, she must have managed to kill Tate. They dump the killing on me, keep her out of it, tell Morey what to say and he says it. So if it's rigged like that, they'll make damn sure I take the fall for it or all their rigging's been wasted. Which means they'll be just as happy if I'm brought in dead."

He nodded decisively. "And with the great American style publicity buildup this whole thing's gotten so far, everyone two-thirds already knows I'm guilty, no questions asked. If I'm brought in a corpse, the case closes up automatically and everyone forgets about it from then on. Cute. All right, it looks like it's gonna have to be Morey first, then Glorieta."

"Who?" Milo asked.

Wilder shook his head. "You don't want to know."

Milo shifted jumpily in his chair. An apologetic smile stirred across his face. "Yeah, sure, Wilder. I wasn't tryna get nosy or nuthin' . . ."

"The less you know about all this, the better for you, Milo."

"Yeah, you're right. They ask me anything, I can't tell them what I don't know, can I? You figuring on pulling that Crescent Club job tonight?"

Wilder stared at him and couldn't keep from laughing. "Are you nuts?"

"I was just wondering, is all."

Amused, Wilder shook his head. "Every cop in the area is on the lookout for me and you think I'm about to pull a stickup? Business as usual?"

Wilder laughed again.

"Didn't you get someone else lined up for it yet? I can give you a few names, if you need them."

"No, that's all right," Milo said. "I'll get somebody. Too late for this week, anyhow. The next big money night at the club isn't till a week from now. It's one night a week or don't bother. None of the other nights is worth the time, even."

Milo stared at the floor and shook his head, sadly. "Too bad," he muttered. "It's a sweet little setup. We could of got maybe fifteen G, if it was the usual Friday night. Maybe more."

"Milo," explained Wilder patiently, "with all the whoop-up going on around town over this Tate bump, it's just as well to let the job go awhile. Next Friday night will be just as good and a helluva lot safer. You got a car?"

"Yeah."

"Get the keys. I'll be taking it."

Milo sat bolt upright. For a moment his eyes looked terrified, but when Wilder only stared impassively at him, he didn't say anything, just went and got the car keys.

"Papers, too," Wilder had to remind him.

Milo brought the keys and registration papers. "You . . . uh, you'll try not to get picked up in it?"

"I'll try." Wilder grinned. "I'll try real hard, Milo, for your sake. Now, I need some money, the more the better. And sunglasses for these eyes. You got any sunglasses?"

"I might have. I'll have to look."

After hunting around awhile, Milo turned up an old pair of sunglasses in a cardboard shoebox on a closet shelf. Wilder tried them. They'd serve. At least they would hide the damage done to his eyes.

Milo brought fifty dollars, mostly in small bills. "That's about all I can manage, Wilder."

He stood there, not looking at Wilder.

Wilder shrugged. "It'll do. Relax, Milo. I'm not going to clean you out. All I need it for is expenses. This isn't the sort of thing I can fix with money, not the kind of money you'd have, anyway."

After another half-hour of waiting, the stuff hanging in the bathroom was dry. Wilder got out of the pants, put on the socks and underwear, climbed back into the pants, and started in on Milo's shirt, slitting it until he could get into it. With the suit coat on over it, he looked alright.

Then he sat down and waited for what was left of the afternoon to die.

Once Milo asked, "Okay if I use the phone? There's some people I got to call."

Wilder shook his head. "Uh-uh."

"Wilder, I still got a living to make," Milo grumbled.

"Make it after I leave."

Sitting on the sofa, smoking and staring out the window, he watched the afternoon gradually turn into evening and finally into night.

CHAPTER SEVEN

Wilder spotted the first pair of watchers the minute he drove Milo's old Chevy past Morey's house. He was ready to find cops on a stakeout, but these weren't cops. They were a type Wilder recognized: sharp dressed, young, good looking, as hard looking as if they'd been finished with varnish.

These two sat in a long dark sedan, which looked as if it could move fast if it had to. One of them was using a cellular phone. That changed things a mite. There wouldn't be any walking in through Morey's front door. Not for awhile, at least.

Cops are easily spotted. On a stakeout like this one, there would only be so many cops: two, maybe three, four at the most. But with this sort of watch, you never knew where the eyes were, because, in a sense, they were everywhere. The invisible eyes of the unknown empire the FBI didn't even know about: volunteer auxiliary helpers on every block in every town and city in the country cooperating with the private dick outfits.

The two Wilder had spotted might be just some of the local sharpsters following the organization's orders. Or private investigators might have been rung in to do the looking, if not necessarily the strong-arm work.

Wilder drove past their parked car, went by Morey's house, turned at the next corner and went a block up toward Main Street, then turned and circled back.

He made the same approach to Morey's street that he had made on the first pass, but this time he stopped in the middle of the next block up and settled in to see what the two watchers were doing, and how long they'd be doing it.

It took a half-hour for Wilder to find out that there were two pairs of watchers. The set he had missed were in another car, parked across the street and down a ways, beyond where Morey lived. One of the men in the first car got out, crossed over and strolled along under the trees, and got into the other car.

That was how Wilder found out about the second car. It was clumsy on their part, but a break for Wilder. Maybe they were confident or just new at this kind of thing. Wilder hoped they were new at it.

A few of the lights were turned on inside Morey's house, but that could be bait. Nobody had moved around inside the house or passed any lighted windows during the time Wilder was watching to see what would develop. It could be that the watchers in the cars had lit the house lights themselves. Morey would be staying on the job at the police station until he got an all-clear signal, before coming on home. Wilder assumed they weren't really expecting him to show, but they were there, in case he did.

The car-hopper left the second car, came back up the street, crossed over, and got back in his own car. The waiting resumed.

Wilder sat watching them awhile, then took out the addresses he had gotten from Milo's phone book to look up Hendricks's address. A mid-block streetlight gave him enough illumination to make out his own handwriting, but when he tried to locate the street on Milo's detailed map of the city, he didn't get anywhere: not enough light for work that fine.

Hendricks might be the nerve center for this whole deal.

Wilder debated whether to leave here and make a stab at locating Bert Hendricks. He knew time was on their side, not his. They could keep gun boys or private snoops sitting on their duffs here or anyplace else for as long as they wanted, but Wilder couldn't sit anywhere, not for long, not with cops looking all over for him. If he stood still, sooner or later one of them was pretty sure to spot him. He decided to try the Hendricks address.

He was about to turn on the ignition when he heard tires squeal up ahead. A car coming from the other direction pulled to a stop beside the car facing Wilder. A man got out of the new arrival and leaned down beside the driver's window of the parked car a moment, then turned quickly and climbed back into his own. The double-parked car backed up until it was clear of the one at the curb. That one drove out, straightened, and started moving, and it really moved. It came tearing up to the corner, slowing only slightly in case there was any cross traffic. There wasn't, so it came straight across the intersection toward Wilder.

He ducked just in time. The headlights blazed above him, filling the inside of Milo's Chevy with a brief glare. The car tore past, its motor growling, low and powerful sounding. At the last second as they went by, Wilder raised his head slightly and peeped, glimpsing the driver and the other man sitting next to him. Once again, the passenger was on his cell phone.

When they were past, Wilder sat up. In the next block, the car that had brought the go message was backing into the parking space left by the departed car. That left two cars still on the watch at Morey's house.

Leaving his lights off for the time being, Wilder whipped the Chevy into the nearest driveway, then backed out into the street, so he was facing the way the big sedan had gone. He could still see its taillights, but the two red dots were getting smaller rapidly with distance.

Braking his reverse momentum, Wilder fought the stick shift into low, and then he was moving forward. But by then he couldn't see red taillights anymore. He pushed the Chevy and drove along the quiet neighborhood street, slowing a bit at each intersection to glance both ways, trying to see if he could find those taillights again, in case the big car had turned off. Nothing. And there was nothing straight ahead, either. After the tenth cross street gave him more nothing, Wilder knew he had lost the car.

Disgusted, he stopped beneath a corner streetlight and examined his map until he knew how to get to where Hendricks lived. It wasn't far from where he was now.

* * *

The Hendricks address turned out to be one of the tall sky-climbing buildings the town had felt called upon to erect. It looked as if it belonged in New York or San Francisco, or at least Edmonton, and faced onto a square park with lots of tall trees in it.

Wilder approached as far as the corner where the park started. He could see the number of the building on a blue canopy stretched across the sidewalk in front of the entrance.

He was looking around for a good place to park when he saw the black sedan that had just lost him back across town in Morey's neighborhood. The sedan was pulled up right in front of the blue canopy.

Backing the Chevy to the curb right at the corner, Wilder stopped next to a johnny pump. He cut his lights, but left the motor running when he saw the big Lincoln's exhaust pipe puffing fumes rhythmically. They might be moving off again at any moment. This time Wilder wanted to be ready.

Nothing stirred.

Sliding across the front seat, Wilder got out on the sidewalk to see if anyone was still inside the Lincoln. He had to go halfway across the side street before he could see that the Lincoln now held only the driver. The other one would be inside the big building somewhere, probably meeting Hendricks.

Back inside the Chevy, he started some more waiting. He didn't have to wait long. One of the sharply dressed types, a big one, came out past the doorman, followed by an older man in a light-colored suit, probably powder blue.

The doorman wasn't quick enough to hold the car door for the second man: the big one already had it open. But the doorman got the front door open for the bruiser and closed it smoothly after him.

Wilder shifted into first gear, keeping the clutch pedal down, watching the Lincoln pull smoothly away from the curb and go zooming down the boulevard between the tall trees in the park and the taller building across from it.

Letting up on the clutch, he pulled out the light switch and hit the floor button to dim the lights. He gave the Chevy plenty of gas. The old car shuddered forward violently and jumped halfway across the side street and stalled.

Wilder took a deep breath, jammed the clutch pedal down again, and braked to a stop. Cutting the ignition, he gave it a beat or two, then turned it on again, and the *ruh-ruh-ruh* of the starter began.

Far up the wide dark boulevard, he could see those familiar red taillights getting smaller and farther away, all over again.

Then they were gone altogether.

He wasn't having any luck at all tailing that Lincoln.

About a minute later, the flooding diminished in the carburetor, and he got the motor running again, but by then there wasn't any hurry at all.

Backing to where he'd been parked beside the corner fire hydrant, he drove forward around the corner and found a parking space a short distance up the side street, opposite the side of Hendricks's building.

Leaving the keys in the ignition, he wiped his prints off the steering wheel, the light switch, the gear stick, the door handles, the keys; all just in case.

Then he walked around to the front of the building.

A cool breeze blew from the park across the way.

Wilder had his sunglasses on before he went under the blue canopy and inside the deep carpeted lobby.

"Good evening, sir." The doorman smiled.

Wilder nodded.

"The Hendricks apartment. I'm expected."

"What name, sir?" the man asked, picking up a phone.

"Floyd. There's more coming too." The doorman nodded and began tapping numbers in.

"Mr. Hendricks left only a few moments ago," he said. "If you had gotten here just a little sooner . . ."

"Yes, he said he might not be here, but he'll be right back. Some kind of emergency meeting. He told us to wait upstairs. Any of the others get here yet?"

"Not yet, sir. Only Mr. Redding is in the Hendricks apartment."

"All right. I'll go on up. Tell Redding I'm on my way, will you?"

Wilder walked on into the lobby.

The doorman called something after him, his voice sharp, but Wilder kept going, turned out of the wide lobby into a bank of elevators and stepped into one.

"Hendricks," he told the operator.

The elevator stopped at the fourth floor.

Wilder was mildly surprised. Somehow, he had expected a man like Hendricks to at least have a penthouse setup.

"Four-C," the elevator man said.

"Thanks."

Across from the elevator, a sign high on the wall had two arrows, one pointing left for "A — G," the other pointing to the right for the rest of the letters.

Without hesitating, Wilder turned left and went along the corridor to the door wearing a metal "4-C."

His finger punched the chime button. They had barely started clanging inside when quick footsteps approached beyond the door and it opened.

A tall wide-shouldered young man with blue-black hair above a handsome tanned face peered up at Wilder.

"Floyd?" he asked. "Since when do we have a Floyd on the—"

"Mr. Redding?"

Redding nodded. His right hand held a short-barreled revolver. His left kept hold of the inside doorknob.

"Morey is sending a couple of us over. He said Mr. Hendricks said something about—"

"A cop wearing sunglasses?" Redding laughed, showing perfect white teeth.

Wilder grinned a little. "We're not supposed to be doing extra-hours work," he explained sheepishly.

Redding's lips still wore the leftovers of the laugh, but he never took his eyes off Wilder. The gun he held wasn't pointed at Wilder, but with the slightest twitch of Redding's wrist, it could be.

"You want to give Morey a call about it?" Wilder suggested. "I can wait out here in the hall . . ."

Redding chewed his lower lip and shrugged. "I guess I'd better. You wait out there."

He started to close the door. He was already turning away when Wilder reached through the narrowing space and clipped him with a quick left.

Redding hit the carpet on his gun-arm side. Wilder slipped into the apartment and got the snub nose out of Redding's hand before he could roll onto his back and get some use out of it. He then went back and shut the corridor door.

Redding sat up. Then he was on his feet. He stared at Wilder with incredulous eyes. After a moment, he threw his head back and burst out laughing.

"Oh, buddy, I wouldn't be you for nothing in the world."

Wilder watched him. When Redding finished laughing, Wilder asked him, "You alone in here?"

"Sure, buddy." Redding smiled. "Sure, I'm alone in here, for awhile. Then . . ." His smile widened. He smacked his right fist into the palm of his left hand. "Then comes the lightning, buddy, and you get yours. Jesus, I wouldn't be you for nothing at all in the wide world. You won't even see tomorrow."

"Maybe you won't even see tonight," Wilder said dryly. "Let's go take a look."

"What?"

"Let's look around. To make sure you're really alone in here."

"Yeah, sure, buddy, that's the way. Push it. You push it real hard. Sure we'll look. Come on, I'll show you the way."

They went through the apartment, checked all the closets, and found no one.

Every so often, Redding would glance sideways at Wilder, grin, and shake his head.

They went out onto a terrace overlooking the park. The terrace reached to the nearby corner of the building. No one was out there.

Wilder herded Redding back inside and sat him on a sofa in the living room.

"So you're Wilder," said Redding cheerfully, still smiling. "The big bad jail breaker!"

"Where'd they go?" Wilder asked him.

"Where'd who go?"

"Hendricks and the big guy with him."

Redding shrugged. "Who knows where they went?"

"You know where they went. Tell me where."

"You think Hendricks tells me where he's going every time he goes out that door?"

"Yeah, that's what I think. Where'd he go?"

Wilder stood in front of Redding, squinting down with his one good eye at the handsome face.

Redding's handsome face wasn't smiling anymore. He stared up at Wilder a long time before he remembered to say something.

"Look, I already told you I don't know where Hendricks went." His voice wasn't cheerfully jeering now. It was soft and husky. Redding heard the husky sound. It jarred him and his eyes got angry. Sharply, he added, "If I knew where, do you think I could tell you? I tell you, then I'm as bad off as you are. Not me, buddy."

"Where'd he go?" Wilder asked again.

"Look," Redding said desperately, "how many times I have to tell you?"

There was a light film of sweat on his forehead and on his upper lip. He swallowed with difficulty. "I don't know where Hendricks went, okay?"

"Yes," Wilder said. "You do know where he went. Where?"

Redding closed his eyes and took a deep breath. When he reopened his eyes, they were bright and angry. His lips were set in a tight stubborn line.

After watching him a moment, Wilder brought the snub nose around in a swift slash.

Redding's head snapped to one side and bounced off the cushioned sofa.

The skin over his right cheekbone was split open. Blood gushed out. The tanned skin of his face was a thin cover for a sick white look underlying it now. His eyes glistened with pain-tears. Some of the tears splashed down his cheeks and fell off his face onto his white shirt and his pin-striped gray suit.

"Where?" Wilder asked again.

Redding set his jaw and shook his head.

Wilder shrugged. "Okay, on your feet."

Redding stood. Wilder pushed him toward the bathroom at the other end of the apartment.

Then the phone rang.

Wilder jerked a thumb at Redding. "Answer it." Redding's face didn't move, but there was a gleam in his eye again. Wilder's eyes narrowed. "Okay, never mind," he said. "I'll answer it."

He picked up the ringing phone in the middle of the fifth ring.

It was the doorman. "Hello, 4-C? May I speak to Mr. Redding, please?"

"Can I give him the message?"

"I'm afraid not, sir. Mr. Redding will have to take it personally."

"Right. I'll get him. Just a minute." Covering the phone mouthpiece with one hand, he told Redding, "The doorman wants to speak to you." He held the phone out. Redding took hold of it, but Wilder held on to it too. "He's checking to make sure everything up here is all right. You tell him everything's fine." Redding's eyes were on Wilder mockingly now, so Wilder added, "Remember, this is your gun, Redding. It can hurt that face of yours a lot worse than I just did. They can only hang me once, so watch what you say."

The gleam in Redding's eyes faded slightly. Wilder released the phone and stood close while Redding murmured, "Hello." After listening a moment, he said into the phone, "No, of course not. It's perfectly all right. Tell Mr. Hendricks when he comes—"

Wilder raised the .38 and held the muzzle right under Redding's nose, shaking his head to caution the hood. Redding stared down into the bore of the revolver for a long second or two before he went on, "—tell him we're waiting for him, in case he needs us." After listening some more, he nodded and said, "Good-bye," and handed the phone to Wilder, who listened, heard the click at the other end, and then hung up.

Wilder nodded approvingly. "That was smart. For a second, I swear I thought you were history."

Suddenly, Redding shuddered. His entire body shook. It took him a long time to stop.

"Out to the can again," Wilder told him.

Redding turned away, snapping over his shoulder, "I told you before, I don't know where Hendricks went. I still don't know where he went."

"We'll see if you don't."

* * *

It took Wilder ten minutes to believe him. Redding really didn't know where Hendricks had gone. Washing his hands in the bathroom sink, Wilder looked down at Redding lying unconscious on the glazed tile bathroom floor. Redding had passed out twice during the questioning. This last one was his third blackout.

When all the blood was off Wilder's hands, he dried them and bent over Redding. Still breathing.

He left the gag in Redding's mouth, checked to make certain the strips of towel binding his wrists and ankles would hold, picked him up, and dumped him in the bathtub.

Listening again and still hearing the sound of Redding's breathing, he left him in the tub the way he'd landed.

Wilder went out onto the terrace to see if it offered an escape route. At the end of the terrace, by the corner of the building, he leaned out over the railing. He could see Milo's Chevy where he'd left it parked, partway up the side street.

There was no way off the terrace.

Going back inside the apartment, he hunted up the service entrance, finding it in the kitchen. He made certain the service door's spring lock was off before he went out to look for a stairway. He found one next to the service elevator, at the end of a short dimly lit corridor.

Alright, the place wasn't too much of a dead-end, anyway.

Returning to the kitchen, he relocked the service door.

It was almost 10:30 when a key was inserted in the front door lock. The doorman downstairs hadn't phoned up, so it had to be Hendricks.

Wilder waited in a little darkened room off the entrance foyer, the Trooper Colt in one hand and Redding's snub nosed .38 in the other.

There had been three men in the Lincoln when it drove off earlier. There might be more of them now.

There weren't.

The door swung inward. A tall, slim, platinum blonde woman stepped inside, closing the apartment's front door softly behind her.

CHAPTER EIGHT

Val!" she called. She walked past the room Wilder was in. He heard her in the living room calling, "Val, honey, are you here?"

Wilder followed her, putting the guns out of sight.

"He is and he isn't," he told the woman's beautifully tailored back. With a startled cry, she spun around.

Her shoulder length pageboy hair swirled, a golden ocean wave looking like one of those television hair commercials they had, except her hair didn't move in slow motion, and her face wasn't quite as pretty as the babes in the ads. Almost as pretty, but not quite.

Something else in her face balanced things out, though — it was a somewhat older and wiser face than any TV chick's could ever get and still show up on television commercials.

"Well!" she gasped. "You surprised me. Are you a new one? Take off those sunglasses, will you? It's night time around here—"

Wilder had forgotten all about the shades. Reaching up, he took them off and slipped them into the breast pocket of his jacket. The woman looked momentarily startled when she saw his left eye. Under the skin of her throat just below the chin, cords appeared, on both sides.

Almost immediately, she got hold of herself and the cords were gone, but not before she had already murmured wonderingly, "Wilder?"

"That's good," he said. "You know me. That means Hendricks must be expecting me."

For a moment, she appeared uncertain. The pupils of her eyes distended slightly. Blinking, she shook her head and smiled quickly.

"Hardly that, Mr. Wilder," she said. "How could I fail to recognize you? They've been showing that face of yours all day: on television, in the evening paper." Shrugging expressively, she turned and began peeling long gloves down her arms. "Oh, yes, that's right," she mused aloud, strolling toward the door that led to one of the bedrooms and the kitchen beyond. "They were beginning to think you might have doubled back up this way and reached town. That was around an hour ago. Up to then, of course, they were spread out all over the countryside down there."

She threw back her head and laughed softly. Stopping in the doorway with a hand on the knob, she smiled at him over her shoulder.

"You've become quite a famous man in this town, Wilder. How in the world did you ever manage to evade—"

"Don't try it, lady." The flat sound of his voice stopped her. She stiffened in the doorway with the door already half-open, one hand still on the doorknob. "Back in here," he ordered.

Her face remained frozen for just longer than a second before she managed to get the smile back on. "I'm only . . . well, I'd like to use the powder room, Mr. Wilder. Did you think I would try to capture you, after all those men couldn't . . .?"

"It's the other way." Her eyes closed. "That's the way to the kitchen," he added, "and the back door." Without a word, she turned and started across the living room toward a door on the opposite side of the main room. Wilder watched her progress and then shook his head. "Forget it, lady. You're staying here."

She halted in the middle of the room and glared at him. "I'd still like to use the . . . the water closet," she said icily. "That is, if I may?"

"No, you may not. No giant steps tonight. Do your business on the rug, if you're in that much of a rush. After I check you out for guns, then maybe you get to use the john, with the door open. You might regret using it, though."

Shrugging and smiling suddenly, she said, "Alright. Here." She tossed her small handbag to him. "Search it," she said. "But hurry, would you? I'm in an embarrassing rush."

Wilder opened the little handbag, saying, "Honey, you haven't been in an embarrassing anything since you were nine." No gun in the handbag. He tossed it back to her. "Face the window," he ordered.

Frowning, she watched him approach.

"Now, listen, big boy," she said past tight lips, "you may have the cops in this metropolis running around in circles, and since you're here, in this apartment, you seem to have a pretty good line on another power-elite — but don't even dream that I'm going to stand still while you run your paws over me with any frisking routine—"

Wilder stopped in front of her and put the .38 away.

"You listen, sister," he said quietly. "I'm a guy who's been pushed out on a high wire ever since I hit this town. There's only two ways I can go: straight ahead or down. Don't bother using any charm on me, or the opposite, either. Turn around. I'm checking you out for hardware. You want it nice? Fine. You want a busted jaw? That's okay too. Take your pick."

She stared up at him, her lips slightly parted. Now she wasn't a woman who knew every trick there was about handling men. Now she was a person, past thirty, and there were microscopic lines near the outside corners of her eyes.

Whatever she saw in Wilder's eyes, she nodded.

"You'd do it too," she murmured.

Turning, she faced the windows and raised her arms. Wilder ran his hands quickly and efficiently over her. There were no weapons.

"Okay, go ahead," he told her. "The can is that way."

"I guess I don't need it anymore."

"I didn't think you did."

"What's next?"

"Next, we wait for Hendricks to get back."

They settled in to wait.

The woman sat on the divan, watching Wilder pace up and down the room. When he went out on the terrace, she stared at his back as he stood at the railing out there, looking down at the park across the street. She didn't move. He came back inside and glanced at her sitting there, watching him.

"What are you to Hendricks?" he asked. He didn't care, but knowing who she was might be a good idea. She had called Redding's first name when she entered the apartment, or somebody's first name. Unless Val was some kind of nickname she used for Bert Hendricks.

"You his wife?"

"Not likely," she laughed. "Not this little girl."

"His woman, though?"

"Call it that. His woman, after being my own woman."

He looked her over. "A pro deal?"

Her lips pressed together. She didn't reply.

Wilder shrugged. "It's nothing to me. I just want to know what you're doing in this apartment."

"I'm often here."

"You in on this?"

"In on what?"

"On my thing," he said, suddenly angry. "This frame, this net they've dropped over me."

"I'm in on nothing," she replied coolly. "I'm for Bert Hendricks because I want to be with him. He has style and he can afford me. He can pay the freight charges and I'm expensive baggage."

"Baggage, anyway," he chuckled.

"Now look—"

"Okay, it's your grapple. What's your name?"

"Why? And what is grapple supposed to mean?"

"Grapple? It means your . . . your racket, your business."

She tasted the word, didn't seem to like the taste, shrugged, and said, "They call me Marge. In this town."

Wilder almost smiled and began pacing again.

After awhile, Marge asked, "Was she worth it?"

Wilder looked at her quizzically. "Was who worth it?"

Marge was studying her hands as they laid out the long gloves on her thighs.

"Glorieta Duncan. Was she worth all this . . . this trouble she brought you?"

Wilder grimaced and shook his head. "No woman is worth any trouble. But she didn't bring me this trouble. I can thank this town's favor givers for all of it."

Smiling wryly, Marge looked up at him. "Don't fool yourself, Wilder. She brought the trouble to you, just as she's done to plenty of other men before you. How was she? In bed, I mean. Was she worth it?"

"Meat's meat," he said, shrugging. "A piece is a piece. You've got a point, though. That husband of hers must be in bad shape, going to the trouble he goes to every time she beats it out the back door for some quick tail. What's wrong with Jeff Duncan, anyway? Can't he find something else, something that'll stay home?"

Marge laughed. "No, it isn't as simple as you think," she explained. "Duncan is old. He's practically senile. He married Glorieta — or rather, she married him — ten years ago. He was old then too, but he was still able to . . . function. But for the last few years he's . . ." She paused, searching for a word, shrugged, then twirled a finger in a circle near the side of her head. "It's kind of funny, in a way, the whole business. It's also kind of nasty too. An old man can act foolishly and viciously, but when the old man can hire other men, the lower class types, to carry out his vicious ideas, it isn't so funny anymore. That's what too much money, too much power can do, even here in the States." She grimaced prettily. "Especially here in the States!"

Wilder listened, nodding occasionally, waiting for her to get to the point. When there turned out to be no point, he said, "Tate was bumped after he left me and Morey in my motel room. From what the two of them said to each other, Tate was taking her home to Duncan, and some local muscle would take me to a lonely place and play handball with my head awhile, and that would wrap things up." He stared at her but she simply went on listening. "I gathered it was a usual routine," he went on, "the method they used to handle the situation each time it came up. Everybody knew what to do because they'd all been through it before."

She smiled and nodded. "Yes, that sounds like the way they'd work it."

"How often does it happen?"

She made a disdainful face. "Each time Hot Pants Glorieta gets that yen? Or each time they catch her at it?"

"I mean how many guys have been given this pile driving? Wasn't there ever any flack afterward?"

"I couldn't give you a number," she replied. "As for repercussions, who would they complain to? The only cop in this city worth a damn is Lt. Bricken, but he would never hear even a rumor about something like this. The rest of them would make sure it never got to him. Oh, he's onto it, I'm sure, but there's not a thing he can do. Wherever he walks, there's a great big silence, paid for in advance, in cash." Marge turned her head and gazed serenely out the wall-wide sliding door window a moment, before going on, "One of these days, if Bricken irritates them too much, he'll probably have an accident too. That handball session you mentioned . . . but he probably won't get to walk away from his." Sighing, she shook her head regretfully. "Perhaps," she added. "And perhaps not. They might not go that far."

Wilder listened closely but there still wasn't anything in it for him.

"So Tate brings her home," he continued with his own thoughts, "and next morning they find Tate dead. She could have killed him."

Startled, Marge looked up at him.

"Glorieta? Not a chance. She couldn't destroy life. She creates life or a reasonable facsimile." She laughed gaily. "She's sort of an earth mother type."

Wilder frowned. "What's that?"

"An earth mother?" Marge smiled slightly. "Oh, it's something nice little boys are always trying to get back to. Or are they nice little girls? One is never quite sure."

Wilder kept staring at her, but he hadn't even tried to follow what she was saying.

"Or the husband," he speculated. "Old Duncan. He could have killed Tate."

"Wilder, what's the difference who did it?" she asked impatiently. "They're looking for you. You did it. You've been chosen."

"Well, I'm damn well going to unchoose myself," he said grimly. "It was Glorieta or the old man. If the old boy's crazy, the way you said, he might have thought Tate was the guy she was making it with and just shot him."

"I suppose he could have," she admitted. "If Duncan actually could shoot a gun with those hands of his shaking the way they always do. And if he could see well enough to hit anything he was trying to shoot." She shook her head positively. "No, Wilder, I don't think Jeff Duncan could do it. Oh, he might want to – that I'll grant you – but with his eyesight as bad as it is, and his hands always shaking . . ." She shook her head again. "No, I can't believe Old Jeff could have managed it."

"Then Glorieta was the one who did it," Wilder insisted, tight-lipped. "She's the only one who could have." Striding over to the sliding glass doors leading to the terrace, he stared out at the night. Nodding, he went on, "Okay, then she's the one I've got to get to. Show me where she lives on this street map."

Gently, Marge shook her head. "Wilder, you're wrong. Glorieta's a no-good slut, but she couldn't kill anyone—"

"Anyone can kill anyone," Wilder said impatiently. "You're hung up on the crap everyone talks about: love your neighbor, keep the peace. But that's just the way the people who run things say people ought to be. It isn't anything like the way people really are. Anyone can kill. It isn't hard at all. Now, where do Duncan and Glorieta live? Point it out to me and hurry. I'm not waiting around for Hendricks anymore. I don't need him. All I need is Glorieta. Where's she at?"

Marge sighed, but she bent over the map and pointed.

"Here," she said, "on Breaker Boulevard, way out, northwest of town, almost as far as the first lake up there. Just west of this end of it, as a matter of fact."

Wilder studied where she was pointing on the map, then straightened, putting the map away.

"First her," he muttered, "then that cop you mentioned, Bricken. Maybe he can straighten it out for me."

"If they let you stay alive that long, Wilder," she pointed out soberly.

"There's no help for that part of it." The phone rang. Wilder glanced toward it, then nodded at Marge. "You better take it."

Laying aside her gloves, she rose from the divan, frowning and eyeing him curiously as she went over to the phone.

Wilder joined her.

"I'll be listening," he reminded her.

"Then answer it yourself," she snapped.

She began to turn away, but he took hold of her wrist and spun her around.

"Marge, sweetie," he growled, "don't go temperamental on me. Pick it up. We've had us a nice neighborly chat up to now. Don't foul it up."

He lifted the phone in the middle of the sixth ring and held it beside her head.

Marge glared at him, but with the phone so close, she blurted out "Hello?" before she could stop herself.

"Marge?" a man's voice said. "Sorry I had to keep you waiting. Is Val there?"

Wilder had bent his head beside hers so he could hear too. When he heard the question, he caught her eye and nodded yes.

"Val's here, Bert," she replied. "Did you want to speak to him?"

Wilder grimaced in disgust and shook his head at her. He pointed toward the bathroom.

Marge frowned, tossed her head irritably, and added hastily into the phone, "He's in the little boy's room right now, Bert. Should I interrupt him . . .?"

"No, it's not that important. Just tell him Riker and Harry will be bringing her over there. They'll use the garage elevator. That one has no operator at night. The fewer people who see her going in, the better, the condition she's in."

"Who . . . who are they bringing, Bert?"

Now Marge wasn't paying any attention to Wilder hovering almost on top of her, with his head pressed close to the receiver. Her eyelids veiled her eyes. Below the fake lashes, she seemed to be examining the tree foliage outside, rustling in the night breeze.

"You know who, Marge," replied Hendricks wearily. "Tell Val. They should be there any minute, so be ready to let them in the service way."

"Aren't you coming with them?" she cried sharply. "Bert, don't hang up. Aren't you going to—?"

"Marge, I can't, not right now." His voice sounded ragged with exasperation. "I've got to stay out here with this old . . . Baby, I'll call you later. Go along with it, will you? Don't give me a hard time on this. It's enough of a mess already. Goddamn that bastard Wilder."

Taking a deep tremulous breath, Marge said, "All right, Bert. Call me. But not here. I'm leaving before they arrive. I don't want to be anywhere near your friend Riker. I can't stand the way he—"

"All right, Marge," the voice said patiently. "But tell Val to be ready for them, okay?"

"Yes, Bert, I'll tell him."

"That's my baby. I'll buzz you at your place, first chance I get. That's a promise."

The line clicked.

Marge held the phone to her ear for another moment. Then, slowly, she hung up. Looking up at Wilder, she studied his eyes and suddenly she shivered.

"What's the matter?" he asked.

"I don't know," she said softly. "All at once, I just got a feeling. I want to get into my car and drive on out of this town, and just go, and keep on going. I want to go so far and so fast that I'll never ever have to hear about anything that happens here from now on."

Nodding, Wilder turned and went over to the divan and picked up Marge's elbow-length gloves.

"That's not a bad idea," he agreed. "If I can't get this rumble squared away pretty quick, there's gonna be some shooting. I'm getting out from under this frame your friend Bert is trying to peg me with, and I'll do it any way I can. I'd prefer to do it the legal way, because they got my fingerprints when they pulled me in last night. So I'd like things nice and regular. But if it can't be done that way, I'll do it the hard way."

Marge crossed her arms in front of her and shook her head. Her hands clutched both elbows, as if for support. Impatiently, she forced herself to stand straighter.

"Well," she said quietly, "first I've got to tell Val. Then I . . . maybe I'll . . ."

Wilder came over to her and stood facing her.

"No," he said. "Forget about Val."

"What?"

Her eyes snapped up to his face. She peered intently into his right eye and at the gleam of his left eye behind the slit in the blue-and-purple shiner.

"What did you do with Val? If you hurt that boy . . ."

Her voice rose almost to a scream.

Wilder grinned. "Relax. Val's in the tub."

"The tub?" Her mouth fell open. She caught her breath and stepped back, staring at him, horrified. "You don't mean you've killed him?"

"Hell, no," Wilder laughed. "He was still breathing okay, last time I saw him."

She studied his face, then turned and started toward the door to the bedrooms and the bathroom. "I'm going to see for myself. I don't believe you—"

Wilder caught her elbows from behind and had her face buried in the divan cushions before she could think to scream. Then one of the long gloves was between her teeth, and it was too late for effective screaming.

Marge struggled, but it did no good. Another brief tussle and the other glove secured her wrists behind her. Releasing her, Wilder stood.

Marge twisted her head, glared up at him, rolled off the divan, somehow got to her feet, and tried to reach the door leading to the bathroom.

Shaking his head in admiration, Wilder brought her back to the divan and dumped her down onto it again, face up this time. He flipped up her skirt.

Her legs reared. She tried to spike him with her heels. Wilder had to grab both ankles quickly, before the heels gouged his face.

"Take it easy," he growled irritably, not smiling now. "I need one of your stockings to lash your feet. Your virginity is safe." Ignoring him, she kept writhing her legs, trying to break free of his hands gripping her ankles.

She had nice legs.

Wilder couldn't help chuckling at all the antics, but when they kept up too long, he became annoyed. "All right," he muttered, "have it, then."

Releasing one of her ankles, he gave her left thigh a short karate chop.

A high, thin sound came from her throat past the gag in her mouth. Her back arched once, convulsively. Tears glistened on her eyelashes. She didn't try any more kicking.

Wilder stripped the stocking from the leg he hadn't given the charley horse to, and used the stocking to fasten her ankles together.

Still bent over her, he pulled her skirt down and, through the skirt, his big hands gently massaged the thigh he'd hurt until some of the agony left her face, and her pain-stiffened body relaxed. Then he left her there and went out onto the terrace.

He wasn't sure how he would work what was coming, when Hendricks's people arrived with Glorieta. Up here in the apartment? Or downstairs in the basement garage? There would probably be a night attendant down there, so perhaps up here would be better.

Leaning on the railing, he looked both ways along the avenue below, but he couldn't see any approaching headlights. Going along the terrace to the end near the corner of the building, he leaned out and peered up the side street. He saw no headlights approaching there, either, but as he turned away, he spotted something else. He took a second look, to be sure, and confirmed his first glimpse.

Wouldn't you know? A squad car was double-parked beside Milo's Chevy!

One of the cops had gotten out and was standing behind it, shining a flashlight beam down onto the license plate.

All the way down the service stairs to the basement garage, Wilder was wondering how long they had been looking for Milo's car.

There was no need to wonder how they had known enough to look for it: Milo had simply turned out to be more scared of Duncan and Hendricks and all the Moreys in this town than he was of Wilder.

And in a way, Wilder couldn't blame him.

CHAPTER NINE

Wilder stood in the dark at the bottom of the service stairs, easing open the door to the garage.

He was grinning, remembering the way Milo had been all afternoon, sweating in that dump of his back there. Then he had been left alone, trying to decide which was the safer way.

When Milo had decided, he had pulled the cross and called the cops. It would be a stolen car report, or something like that. The description Milo gave them of the car thief couldn't miss. All Milo had to do was mention the shiner Wilder was wearing. Opening the door the rest of the way, Wilder slipped through into a dimly lit basement corridor. One way was the service elevator. The other had a door with "GARAGE" stenciled on it in black.

Wilder went that way, thinking Milo might have made the right choice. Maybe Milo was smarter betting against Wilder. Then again, Milo could turn out to have guessed dead wrong. Wilder laughed softly.

If it turned out Milo had, this would be one of the sorriest days Milo ever saw.

There wasn't much light in the garage. When Wilder got the door open and slipped through, pulling the door quickly shut behind him, the brief band of light behind him seemed as bright as a beacon blazing into seemingly utter darkness.

He got the door shut and crouched beside it, dismayed at the hollow echo the slight sound set off.

Holding his breath, he peered around, giving his eye time to get used to the dimness.

At the far end of the vast space, near the street ramp, was a small glass-enclosed office with a light on inside. A man emerged from the little cubicle and stood in the middle of the wide open ramp leading outside, staring back his way. Wilder remained motionless and waited to see if the attendant would investigate.

The man stood still awhile, but not hearing anything more, he went back inside his little office. Wilder started up that way. His shoes whispered on the concrete underfoot.

A double row of cars bulked in the gloom down the middle of the long garage. Another row was nosed into the wall on the left.

Carefully, Wilder worked his way along the length of the underground garage until he was near enough to the entrance cubicle to see the attendant tilted back in a wooden chair, his eyes closed.

Leaving the man to his snooze, Wilder moved silently up and down the rows of cars, getting the layout of the place. He soon saw that there was no sense trying to find the Lincoln's parking slot, since there were no markers or apartment numbers marking which tenant had which slot. He didn't even know if the Lincoln was kept here. It might belong to the man who had been driving it.

When he knew what was where in the parking garage, Wilder decided to stay out of sight about midway down the length of the place until the Lincoln he had seen out front earlier arrived with Riker and his buddy — and Glorieta Duncan. Then he'd have to see what the situation looked like before he tried anything. If he tried anything.

He wondered what those squad car cops were doing around now.

Headlights outlined the wide garage ramp. Wilder ducked behind the car he had been leaning against.

The car behind the headlights drove down through the entranceway.

The attendant emerged from his glass office and spoke to the driver. Wilder couldn't make out what was said, just whispering echoes.

The car came into the garage and drove down the left side between the blank wall and the center double row of cars. The attendant went back to his catnapping.

Staying low, Wilder watched until the car's headlights were almost lighting his face. Then he ducked and crouched until the car drove by.

Slipping between two cars, he emerged into the open and sprinted after the car toward the elevator end of the garage.

Close to the elevator entrance, the new arrival slowed and turned into one of the unoccupied center slots.

The moment the car came to a halt and the motor was killed, Wilder had to stop running. His footsteps would have made too much noise in the silence. He kept going, though, moving carefully on his toes, trying to keep the whispering sounds his shoes made on the concrete from getting too loud.

Which way to work it? The driver first? Or the other one? He'd have to get closer.

Wilder paused a moment, watching the car's occupants until he was sure none of them had spotted him. Then he ducked across a couple of unoccupied parking slots and slipped between two cars just down from them.

He grinned, thinking all this cat-footing might be a waste if this was the wrong car. There were a lot of tenants in a building this big.

It wasn't the wrong car. One of them said, "Okay, Mrs. Duncan, everybody out. End of the line."

The door on the driver's side clunked shut. Keys jingled.

Wilder took out Redding's .38 and held it by the barrel in his left hand for slugging work.

Still staying in a crouch, he moved one car closer.

One of the men was leaning into the back of the car. Inside it, muffled and low, he was saying, "Don't give us no trouble now, Mrs. Duncan. It won't help anything at all."

A woman's voice replied. Wilder couldn't make out whatever she said, but he recognized Glorieta's voice. It sounded scratchy again.

The man was helping her out of the car. He shut the back door a moment after her heels clicked on the concrete.

Emerging from between the parked cars, she stopped a few feet from where Wilder was hunkered down, her back to him.

Wilder sank a bit lower.

A big man came around the car and stood beside her, looming against the lesser darkness of the garage ceiling, behind and above him. He put a hand on Glorieta's shoulder and began guiding her toward the door leading to the elevator.

She stumbled. From the far side of their car, the other man came into sight and reached out to steady her. "Easy, Riker," he chuckled. "You don't know your own strength."

"She isn't half as drunk as she's pretending," Riker growled.

"Get her moving, Harry. We haven't got all night."

As the second man turned away with Glorieta, Wilder rose and closed in on Riker from behind, moving on his toes.

Riker must have heard something, because he started to turn. Wilder gave him the gun butt on the back of his head.

Riker gasped but he stayed on his feet.

Wilder followed him up when he staggered a step. He swung the .38 a second time.

Riker's head lowered a little. Both his shoulders rose, bunching, as if he was trying to protect his head with them.

Wilder could hear Riker's breathing. It sounded like a wounded hippo panting.

The man with Glorieta turned his head and looked back.

"What's the matter?" he called.

Wilder grimaced. This Riker had a hard head. Two on the skull and he was still on his feet.

When Riker didn't respond, Harry shrugged and went on leading Glorieta toward the elevator corridor.

Riker was so big a man that apparently Harry hadn't noticed Wilder behind him. But Wilder knew he couldn't stay lucky much longer.

Pulling out the long-barrelled Trooper Colt, he jammed a heel-kick into Riker's left leg, just behind the knee. When Riker dipped to his left at the start of a rushing headlong fall, Wilder brought the Trooper around in a full swing. The barrel slammed against Riker's skull. This time Wilder made sure the barrel hit Riker's hat. Otherwise, the slugging would certainly cave in even a skull as hard as Riker's. Wilder wanted this bruiser out cold, not dead.

That last one did it.

Riker hit the concrete heavily and lay there without moving. Pausing to make sure he was out, Wilder then slipped past him and went in low on the other one.

Glorieta turned her head and saw Wilder coming up behind them. She cried out with surprise and fright. Her escort turned to look, still unable to see much in the dimness.

Wilder caught a glimpse of metal as the man brought a gun out from under his coat, but by then he was on top of him.

He jammed the Trooper into the man's middle.

"Don't do a thing," he whispered.

There was no way for Harry to do anything, even if he had wanted to. The muzzle of the Colt punched the breath out of him. He bent forward, gasping with pain. His hand still held the gun, though.

Wilder chopped the butt of the big Trooper down at the man's gun hand. Gleaming metal spun away. The weapon hit concrete somewhere and went scraping over toward a corner.

Harry staggered back, trying to crab walk to the door leading to the elevator. Wilder grabbed him and spun him around.

"Don't," Harry gasped. "I'm—"

"The car keys," Wilder hissed softly.

"Yeah, yeah, car keys," Harry murmured. He was staring down at the big revolver Wilder still held pointed at him.

Without looking at her, Wilder said, "Get back in the car, Glorieta."

"Who . . . who is it?"

"Dan Wilder," he replied impatiently. "Get in the car. Hurry."

He put the Trooper away, took out the .38 again, and waited while Harry managed to fumble the car keys out of one of his pockets. Grabbing them, Wilder turned to make certain the other one, Riker, was still out.

He was. He just lay there facedown on the concrete. A brawny bastard, even flat out that way.

"Come on," Wilder said. "Over here."

He quickly frisked Riker, keeping the .38 ready in his hand, just in case Harry got any ideas. His searching fingers found what felt like a .45 semi-automatic in a sling holster.

Skittering it off along the concrete floor under the nearest parked cars, he turned back to Harry, still bent over slightly, holding his stomach.

"Grab this guy," Wilder ordered. "Come on, grab him. Pull him clear so I can back your car out."

"Yeah, sure, mister," Harry said. He reached down and took Riker under the arms.

"No, not that way," Wilder said. "Grab his wrists. We'll be at it all night like that."

"Oh, sure," Harry said eagerly. "I see what you mean."

Suspicious, Wilder glanced at him. Harry was awfully agreeable for a guy who had just taken a gut gouge.

They started dragging Riker across the concrete.

"Over to that door," Wilder gasped, pausing for a short breather.

Turning his head slightly, he saw Glorieta still standing where he'd last seen her.

Cursing under his breath, he went over to her and growled, "I told you to get in the car."

"Is it you, Danny?"

Her voice sounded funny, slow-thick. Wilder smelled liquor. She'd been doing some drinking and the stuff was still with her.

"Yes, it's me."

Putting away Redding's .38, he led her over to the car. She moved easily, but listlessly.

When he opened the front door on the passenger side, she asked, "Are you coming with me?"

"Yeah. Get in."

She climbed inside. Wilder slammed the door shut and went over to see how the Riker-moving was proceeding.

Harry had hauled the huge bulk of Riker almost over to the door leading to the elevator corridor, so Wilder went in there ahead of him and punched the elevator button.

"Bring him on in here," he called cautiously.

Harry had left off dragging Riker and was peering through the open doorway at Wilder.

"I said bring him in here," Wilder repeated.

"Oh, yeah, sure," Harry said hurriedly.

Harry was panting from his exertions. Bending down, he got a fresh grip on Riker's thick wrists and hauled. Droplets of sweat fell from his straining face. He kept licking his lips.

From the other end of the parking garage, the attendant called something, setting echoes loose. Wilder could only make out what sounded like "Alright back there . . .?"

Going back into the garage again, Wilder stood where he could keep an eye on his agreeable prisoner and still see along the line of parked cars to the attendant's lighted cubicle at the far end.

"Harry, tell him everything's great," Wilder said quietly.

Harry straightened, nodded, and called out, "It's okay, George. Good night."

The attendant replied, maybe saying good night, maybe anything, and went back inside his little glass enclosed office.

"Okay," Wilder said, "let's get this guy into the elevator."

To speed things up, Wilder grabbed one of Riker's wrists. Together, they hauled the big man into the corridor and along the short distance to the elevator. The doors were just sliding open when they came grunting up to it.

Hauling and shoving, they managed to get Riker inside. Pushing the fourth floor button, Wilder held the doors open a moment and told Harry, "Don't stop this thing until you reach four. I'll be watching that dial down here." He pointed up at the circular floor indicator, whose arrow pointed at the B.

"I won't stop it . . ." Harry began to assure him.

Wilder didn't listen, just stepped back and permitted the doors to close and the elevator to begin its journey upward.

When he returned to the garage, the attendant was still in his cubicle by the entrance ramp.

When Wilder slid behind the wheel of the Lincoln, he had the car keys ready. Starting the motor, he glanced across at Glorieta.

She sat quietly, her white face placid, her hands relaxed and folded on a long, pale leather bag in her lap. She wore a light-colored topper with a big collar turned up in back.

She didn't look at him when he got in beside her.

Backing the Lincoln out of its parking slot, Wilder started it gliding soundlessly toward the distant exit ramp. He could see the attendant rising from his sleeping chair as the Lincoln approached.

Leaving the headlights off, Wilder increased his speed a bit.

The attendant emerged from his glass-walled box just as the Lincoln came rolling up to it.

"Forgot your lights, Mr. Riker," the man called out. Wilder pulled out the light switch, grinning.

"Thanks, pal. There's your lights."

The brights came on. The attendant squeezed his eyes shut for a second against the sudden glare.

A second was all Wilder wanted. He goosed the gas pedal. The Lincoln shot past the man and swooped up the ramp and across the wide sidewalk to the street.

That was one less person who could identify him, Wilder was thinking. Not that it mattered much by now.

Easing the Lincoln onto the street, he turned left, up toward the park and the front of the building. At the corner, he slowed to make a right turn.

He wasn't sure where those two squad car cops had gotten to, and he didn't want to go driving past the front of Hendricks's building and maybe pass right in front of them and the doorman.

But he hadn't even begun his turn when he heard a shout back by the blue canopy. In the rearview mirror, he saw the doorman pointing.

A cop came running out onto the road, tugging at his gun holster and yelling.

Cutting the wheel hard to the right, Wilder gave the Lincoln gas.

"Go ahead, stall on me, you bastard!" he snarled at the car. "Make everything perfect."

The Lincoln wasn't a staller, though. It leapt forward and seemed to flatten out powerfully as the speed increased, the way a greyhound gets closer to the ground as it hits its stride.

Passing wind roared outside.

Far to the rear, Wilder thought he heard the crack of a shot, but he didn't hear anything hit the car, so he didn't worry about it.

Four blocks up, he slowed a bit to turn west, away from Thomaston's main drag.

Beside him, Glorieta sat placidly, staring serenely ahead.

The streets were mostly deserted. No one was out walking at this late hour. Wilder glimpsed only an occasional car, over toward the center of town. Farther out, no cars moved.

Only high silver streetlights were alive in the night.

Most of the houses crouched in their yards were dark, but for a moment Wilder imagined that he could hear the houses breathing, patient and slow and bulky, just beyond where the harsh streetlights reached.

Turning off the Lincoln's headlights, he cut his speed considerably. Without the lights, these residential parts of town appeared almost eerie. The all-but-silent motor under the hood was the only sound Wilder could hear besides the woman's soft breathing beside him.

Off in the night, back the way they'd come, a siren sounded, a plaintive wailing doleful cry in the summer night.

Overhead, the sickle moon in the sky was thicker than it had been the night before, when it had shone on Glorieta outside the bar where he had picked her up.

Tonight the moon gave more light, too much light to suit him. It helped driving without lights, though: he could see whatever he needed to see, with the moon and the spaced streetlights, provided he kept his speed down. Only on older streets, where big trees on both sides of the road were more heavily foliaged above, was driving without lights tricky. The trees blotted out most of the moonlight and only let trickles of the streetlights guide his way.

Another distant siren sounded off to the right. A few blocks farther on, a third screeched somewhere, from the north this time.

"Almost a full surround," Wilder noted quietly into the silence.

Shaking his head, he grinned ruefully. "No place to go anymore. They'll be up ahead of us any minute, too."

Glorieta turned her head and looked at him. After studying his face a moment, she leaned forward so she could see his swollen left eye. Wilder glanced at her, then returned his attention to his driving.

"What are you gaping at?" he asked irritably when he almost clipped a tree along a curved stretch of the road.

"Dan," she whispered, "what did they do to your face?"

Startled at the concern in her voice, he looked at her again. She was staring at him in the faint reflection of the silver light outside. Around her eyes, he caught a glint of light reflected from tears.

"More than I can remember," he replied harshly. "You're damn solicitous now, aren't you? When Tate was riding you about me last night, you weren't bothered one bit. And you knew what was going to happen to me next, didn't you?"

Her fingers clutched his right arm. "Dan, don't you know I didn't mean anything I said? I had to say that to—"

"Quit grabbing my arm," he snapped, shoving her hand away with his elbow. "I'm trying to drive this thing."

She didn't reply. Sliding along the seat to the far end, she sat there in the corner, watching him, her face in shadow.

Then, her voice husky, and with the merest trace of the familiar scraping sound back in it, she said, "I thought at the time that if I . . . if I pretended I didn't care what they did to you . . . they might not hurt you so much . . ."

He nodded absently and shrugged. "No difference, now. The damage is done."

"There is a difference," she cried. "Dan, I wouldn't hurt you. I want you to . . . to love me."

He laughed. "Sorry, Glorieta baby. I'll have to disappoint you. Your husband and his friends don't seem to want me around anymore."

Cocking his head to listen, his mouth set grimly. Another siren had joined the rest from somewhere ahead and to the left. It sounded nearer than any of the others.

"Hear that? They want this guy's gut-blood, honey. And it looks like they'll be able to get it too."

"They frighten me," she said gently. "Sirens always frightened me. They seem to fill the world with their screaming. Why don't they stop . . .?"

"Sirens frighten you?" he said mockingly. "It's my gizzard they're after, not yours. Why should they frighten you? All you did was start this whole business rolling."

Glorieta's head ducked under the impact of his words. Turning away, she gazed out the window on her side at the lines of cars parked on the quiet streets they were driving along.

Suddenly she cried, "Dan, couldn't you find a parking place along one of these streets? With all these cars, surely the police won't be able to find just one car."

He shook his head. "No good."

"Oh, Danny! Why not?"

"How many Lincolns do you think they've got in a town like this?"

"I don't know. Does that make any diff—?"

"It means they can find this one easy because there aren't that many others to confuse them. All of them have this heap's license number by now. If they don't spot us in the next five minutes, cruising, they'll know we've gone to ground and parked somewhere, trying to wait it out. So they'll begin a systematic street-combing, slow and steady and surer than hell. Every off-duty cop in this town can be brought in on it. If they use their own cars, not police squad cars, we'll never know who's passing us, off-duty cops, or just plain citizens. Hell, they can even use the regular radio programs to tell everyone in town to stay off the streets. Inside an hour, they'll put the arm on us."

Discouraged, Glorieta nodded. "Yes, I suppose you're right," she murmured.

"Then they'll have me on a kidnapping charge too," Wilder laughed. "Not that they need any more charges, but I guess the more the merrier."

"But why stay in the city, Dan? Why not just drive on out of town? Then they can search all they want to—"

"Great advice," he jeered. "Except which way is out? Which road do I take? Which one is a through street and which a dead-end? Those cops know every street in this town. They ought to: they patrol them eight hours a day, every day. I don't even know if this street we're on right now is a dead-end half a block from this next intersection."

"I know where it goes, Dan. Stay on it. Go straight ahead."

Her voice was different now. She didn't sound fuzzy anymore, or too excited and emotional, either. She was leaning forward, peering ahead through the windshield.

Flicking a quick glance at her, Wilder hesitated, then nodded and returned his attention to the road ahead. "Okay," he agreed. "Maybe you do, at that. You sure as hell ought to know it better than I do."

Past tight lips Glorieta said, "I know this town better than anyone. I've spent enough afternoons doing nothing else but drive around this lousy city. That's all I was allowed to do — go for drives. I think I know every street in Thomaston. I've driven down them often enough!"

Wilder nodded. It made sense. "Okay, maybe this isn't a lost cause after all."

"Turn right at this next corner," she ordered.

"That looks like a dirt road."

"It is a dirt road."

"Now look, doll, don't get me hung up on some half-mile long dirt-farmer's driveway—"

"Turn into it, Dan," she said urgently. "It's a through road. It'll get us past any roadblocks they might set up on the paved roads out this way. Trust me."

He still hesitated before committing the Lincoln to the dirt road. But since he had nothing better to suggest, he did as she advised, swinging the big Lincoln into the dirt track.

The tires immediately began throwing gravel against the underside of the car.

Up to now, his speed had been barely more than a crawl, what with driving without the headlights on, so he didn't have to reduce his speed much further to allow for the dips and creases in the composition surface of this track.

"There's one of them," she murmured.

Wilder looked where she was pointing. Across a field to the left, a red light revolved atop a police car.

Glorieta slid closer to him.

"That's a highway patrol car," she whispered.

"So they're in on it too," he said disgustedly.

He felt her warm hand on his knee.

"They've all been on the lookout for you since morning," she said, turning her head and peering up at him.

"Dan, I don't understand how you've managed to stay clear this long."

"I've got pull with the higher-ups in local politics." He grinned sardonically.

She half-smiled and faced forward.

The Lincoln wallowed and bumped along. The dirt road was getting rougher to travel on and the angle it was taking them on seemed to be bringing them closer to the roadblock patrol car off to the left.

Wilder mentioned that.

"Up ahead is a fork," Glorieta reassured him. "It's a pretty poor road, the right fork, but I've been over it in my convertible, so this car should be able to deal with it. Anyway, it's better than taking the other fork. That would take us too close to where that car is stopped."

Wilder nodded. "Okay, we take the right fork. If it doesn't work out, well . . . we can worry about that at the time."

"There it is, just ahead," she said.

She alerted him just in time. He would have missed the turnoff if she hadn't pointed it out to him. He had to bring the Lincoln almost to a complete stop before starting to make his turn and easing into the new road.

Then the rough part really began.

There were rocks in the road and deep ruts where many wheels had passed along it through the years. Grass grew on the hump between the ruts, sticking up at all angles, tall and thick. Sometimes small bushes grew there too. Wilder sweated the Lincoln over them carefully, and the bigger rocks too, feeling those scrape against the guts of the car underneath. It felt as if a rasp was scraping his own bones.

"All we'd need right about now," he panted, wrestling the steering wheel, " . . . bust the pan . . . or rip the muffler loose. They'd hear us a mile away."

"It's all right, darling," she whispered. "You're doing wonderfully. There's one, Dan. Watch out for that rock. Better angle your right wheels up onto the middle—"

"If I can get them up onto it," he complained. "Where did you ever dig up this monster of a road?"

Somehow, they got past the dangerous stretch, the big car sliding past the boulder as if it were a ship slipping past shoals in a treacherous sea. The road climbed on, tilting upward, then downward in sudden dips, fantastically steep in places.

"This Indian trail must have been great for the old Model Ts," Wilder gasped.

He eased and bulled and breathed the Lincoln up steep slopes and down their far sides, then up others, and still more after those.

The track seemed to go on endlessly.

Branches whipped against the sides of the car in places where bushes and shrimpy trees had grown close to both sides of the track, overhanging it with their shrubbery. The car bent them aside, thrashed along corridors between them, and at last burst free on their far sides.

Whenever the taller trees closed overhead, there was hardly any moonlight to go by, but Wilder still didn't dare use the headlights. Everything around was pitch-black.

Headlights in here would show a long way off to anyone watching. And those cops would be watching.

Finally, beside him, Glorieta sighed and leaned back. "We made it, Danny." Her hand patted his leg and she laughed. "The worst is behind us."

"Ahuh. So where are we?"

"Up ahead is a county road. Turn right onto that. I think I know where we can go where they'll never find us."

"Where's that?" Wilder asked, squinting ahead for the county road.

The woods they were crawling through now were thinner. More of the moonlight got through to light the way ahead. "On my husband's estate."

Wilder stabbed a quick disgusted glance at her. He barely got his eyes back on the road ahead in time to jam on the brakes. The county road swept across the end of the dirt road they'd been traveling along. Beyond the paving straight ahead was nothing but fields, pale in the moonlight.

"Great!" he sneered. "Your husband's place! Now let me think of one. How about the parking lot outside the state penitentiary? Or the governor's front lawn?"

"Danny, you don't understand," she protested. "The grounds are enormous. At the north end, Jeff built a lake-side lodge. We used to go there, the first few years we were married, for privacy. We'd walk. No road leads to it from the main house but there's another way in. Kind of a service road for deliveries. If we follow this road to the right, we'll avoid the patrols. They'll never imagine you know about this back road, let alone the service road into the lodge." Wilder listened closely. It didn't sound bad.

"I have a key for the gate," she went on. "Once we're inside the estate, it's less than a mile from the gate to the lodge itself."

Wilder sat there thinking it over. Night insects clicked and buzzed in the darkness outside the car.

Glorieta made the lodge sound like a sensible place to hole up. Once again, he knew he didn't have anything to top it.

"It doesn't sound bad," he finally admitted.

"Just for tonight, Dan."

He got the Lincoln moving again, turning onto the fine gravel county road and heading north, still without headlights. No trees overhung this road, so the thick sliver of moon gave sufficient light to allow him to pour on a bit more speed.

"Tomorrow too," she added thoughtfully, "if we stay there that long. Then, tomorrow night, we can—"

"We?"

She looked up at him. Her hand gripped his leg hard. "Yes, we. If you'll take me with you—"

Wilder burst out laughing. "Well, I'll be a cross-hatched monkey's uncle. One night you as good as feed me into a meat grinder, and the next you want to go a-roving with me, while half the cops in creation are running around sniffing like pointers, trying to zero in on me for murder in the first, and murdering a cop, to boot. Glorieta, baby, you take the ticket, sure enough."

"Dan, please don't talk like that," she begged. "You are the only chance I've got. You're not afraid of Jeff or Hendricks. You're the only man I've ever seen who isn't scared of all of them put together—"

"The hell I'm not," Wilder objected. "Baby, I know better than to believe this money-crazy country we're in is really a free country. It's free unless someone with real dough decides to point the human scum who are always for hire at you. Then it stops being a free country real quick, and no laws and no cops and no anybody can protect you from that."

"But Dan, you can get me out of this town," she went on as if she hadn't heard a word he'd said. "I've tried to get away, but they always found me and brought me back. I could never get clear of this place. Once, he even had me put in a sanitarium. He had me committed. Isn't that ironic?" She laughed. There was a note of hysteria in the laugh. Her fingernails bit through Wilder's pant leg. "My husband belongs in one himself," she went on. "They have to spoon feed him. It's that Hendricks. He keeps Jeff propped up in that big house just so he can sign papers whenever Hendricks wants them signed. Sometimes I think Bert Hendricks keeps Jeff alive through sheer willpower, forces him to keep breathing, and swallowing, and taking those shots, just so he can keep signing papers . . . and year after year the money disappears, faster and faster—"

"Okay, calm down," Wilder interrupted. "Let go of my leg. Your nails feel like they're drawing blood."

Surprised, she glanced down at her hand and jerked it hastily away from his leg.

Taking a deep shuddering breath, she leaned wearily back in the seat beside him, murmuring, "Don't be angry with me, Dan. If only you could get me away from here! Just keep them from sending me back, even if it's only for a little while. As soon as you think they won't be able to find me, you can leave. Anywhere, anytime you feel like going off on your own, you can. I don't want to get in your way, Dan, I really don't, but . . . you're the only hope I've got . . ."

"Some hope!" he growled. "A walking death house candidate."

". . . and if I don't get away from that sadistic old maniac soon, I'll really go out of my mind," she wailed desperately. "I'll end up in a sanitarium again and this time I'll need it. And if that happens, I'll never get out . . ."

"Okay, we'll talk it over later," he said hurriedly. "First, let's get back to this secret way into your estate. You say you've got a key to some gate, so getting inside shouldn't be a problem. But what happens when we get to the lodge you mentioned? Is there a garage where we can stash this Lincoln? Or thick woods nearby it'll fit under and stay out of sight?"

"There are lots of trees right behind the lodge. We can leave it in among them. No one will be able to see it. No one ever goes there, except me . . ."

"Okay, then we're alright with the car."

"Jeff never wanted any cars out there," she explained apologetically. "That's why there's no garage. He wanted privacy, just the two of us." She laughed bitterly. "He was still . . . sane, then. It's only the last four or five years that he's gotten . . ."

She stopped speaking, shook her head hopelessly, and peered out at the ghostly countryside fleeing past beside the road.

"If the old bastard wanted privacy so much," Wilder asked, "how come there's this driveway a mile long going in from that back gate we're headed for?"

"I told you before," she said. "Didn't I? That was for deliveries. And for the servants."

Wilder chuckled. Okay, he'd asked and she'd answered.

She began talking again, pouring it out: about her marriage and how her husband had changed in the last few years.

Wilder didn't bother to listen. He always ran into this with women. He could never get them to quit babbling about their miserable marriages.

Sometimes he wondered why the hell any of them bothered getting married in the first place. None of them seemed to get much out of it, except things to bitch and whine about.

Perhaps that was why they needed marriage — for ammunition; something to gripe about.

After awhile, he became aware that Glorieta wasn't complaining anymore. She must have run out of material.

Or maybe she was organizing new stuff.

He let her be and drove gratefully on in the silence through the pale moonlight.

CHAPTER TEN

The slice of moon was halfway down the southwestern sky when Glorieta told Wilder to turn off the county road and go east along a private asphalted lane.

Buzzing past them on the right as they went was a high chainlink fence. “There’s the gate,” she said, pointing ahead.

Turning in, he stopped short of the high steel wire gate. Beside him, Glorieta dug around in her bag and brought out a wafer-shaped leather key holder. Getting out of the car, they went over to the gate.

Wilder lit a cigarette and held the match so she could find the right key in the bunch.

Inserting it, she turned it in the lock.

Overhead, Wilder heard a click and a brief buzzing sound. He looked upward. The slight noises seemed to be coming from a small box-like affair rigged atop one of the steel gateposts. A black strand of wire or cable ran from the box into tree-darkness beyond the fence.

When Glorieta got the gate unlocked, Wilder helped her push it open. It was well-balanced and moved easily.

“What’s that thing?” He pointed up at the box, visible against the star-dotted sky.

“Probably some kind of alarm,” she said. “In case anyone climbs the fence or tries tampering with the gate.”

"It's still going," he said. "I can hear it buzzing."

She shrugged. "Maybe it's always going."

Reluctantly, Wilder nodded. "Okay, I guess," he said, still unhappy about it. "After I drive through, you better close the gate. If I do it, I'm liable to do something wrong and set that alarm off."

"All right, Dan."

Getting back behind the wheel, Wilder drove through the gateway and a bit beyond, to give her clearance to swing the gate shut behind the Lincoln. He heard it close with a soft clang. Then she was back beside him, closing the door on her side and sliding across to sit close against him.

He started forward slowly, still without headlights. He could feel the warmth of her body when the car's movement tilted her against him.

It wasn't quite a mile to the lodge: Wilder clocked it.

Off through some trees on his left, he got moon-glimpses for the last few hundred yards. Then they emerged from the woods and there ahead of them was the lodge, perched atop the steep western shore of a narrow lake.

Moonlight sparkled and glittered delicately on the moving water beyond the rustic looking building.

Wilder stopped the car and from a distance studied the dark lodge awhile. The only sound he could hear was the purr of the Lincoln's idling motor.

"It looks empty," he said quietly. "Can you get inside?"

"Yes. I have a key for here too. I've got all kinds of keys, for getting into all sorts of places around here. It's the key to get out I can't get hold of."

"Ahuh."

Carefully, he backed the Lincoln in under the trees at the edge of the woods and killed the motor.

"I'll work it back deeper under these trees in the morning," he told Glorieta as they got out. "This will do for the night."

Coming around the car, she took his hand.

Wilder squinted down at her as they started toward the lodge. She was overdoing this loving-kindness routine. Still, she wanted something from him, so he might as well let her think she was going to get it.

A U-shaped porch ran around three sides of the lodge, leaving only the landward side to rise straight up from the pine needle covered ground clear to the roof beam. The base of the U on the lakeside was wider than the two ground level side stems, and it was built out over the edge of the lake like a split log balcony.

They went into the shadows beneath the porch roof on the north side of the lodge and turned the corner of the structure onto the bigger part hanging above the water. A cool breeze drifted the smell of the lake up to them.

While Glorieta was picking the door key from among the others in her key holder, Wilder listened to the lapping sounds the lake made beneath the porch flooring.

The moonlight didn't reach where they were, so she was having a difficult time finding the right key.

Wilder tried to relax. He forced himself to watch the silver antics the moonlight was performing on the dancing water.

Far off down the lake a tiny light burned, but it was too distant to look like anything but a pinpoint. That was the only light he could see.

Behind him, the cabin door creaked on its hinges when Glorieta pushed it open. She hesitated outside on the porch until Wilder went past her and entered the dark doorway.

Inside, the darkness was lessened slightly by some of the moonlight shining through windows in the south wall. The place smelled damp, unused, woodsy.

"It has only two rooms," Glorieta whispered beside him. "We can sleep in this room. It's a bedroom-livingroom. I'll get sheets and blankets."

There she went with that "we" again. It gave Wilder the itch, but he shrugged the feeling off. He was tired, and a piece was a piece.

He wondered if the only thing that was really on her mind was getting her rocks off again before Hendricks and his crew dragged her back to her husband.

"Any food here?" he called.

From a corner closet she said, "No. We always had food brought down."

"Figures," he muttered. "How about hot water?" There was water available in the back room from an electrically operated pump. Luckily old Duncan hadn't given that feature any rustic treatment by putting in some kind of crank-well, which spared Wilder the necessity of pumping water by hand. After he turned the fuses around in the fuse box, he drank three glassfuls of tap water; his stomach had to be satisfied with that. It wasn't food but it was better than nothing.

Returning to the front room, he found Glorieta standing in the moonlight which shone through one of the south windows.

She was down to her slip. As he watched, she pulled it over her head and laid it on top of her coat and dress on the floor. Looking up, she saw him standing there in the dark watching her.

"Hello," she said softly, smiling at him. Her eyes were shining. Her teeth seemed to catch pearl glow from the quarter moon pouring silver light through the window behind her. "I love you so much, Danny. I never loved anyone so much, never."

I'll bet, he thought. "Look, chicken," he said carefully. "I've got to ask you some questions. I have to find out what happened last night."

She bent to unfasten her garters, but with her head still lowered, she paused. After a moment, she went on removing the first stocking. When it slid down her leg, her hands went to the other one, but they only loosened the fastening on one side. Then she looked up, her heavy black hair swinging on both sides of her face. He couldn't see her eyes anymore.

"Dan?" she said, loosening the remaining fastener on the garter and letting that stocking slide down too.

"What?"

"Are you saying . . . do you mean you didn't go there to Hendricks's place to get me away from his men?"

Wilder nodded grimly."I was afraid that was what you thought."

She straightened and stood there in the patch of moonlight, staring at him.

Now he could see her eyes again. They filled with sudden tears. "Danny, do you mean you don't want to love me?"

"What the hell's that got to do with anything?" he snarled. "Can't you get it through that skull of yours that I'm under the gun? This whole area is crawling with law on the lookout for me for doing a hit I couldn't have pulled off, and all you can think about is whether I want to put the blocks to you . . ."

Violently, she turned her head from side to side, as if she was trying to escape hearing his words. Some of her tears went sailing off, with silver moonlight dots riding on them until they flew into the shadows on each side of the window behind her.

Whirling, she stooped and picked up her clothes. When she faced him again, she held them in front of her, coat and all. "No, you don't want to love me," she wailed. "Alright, I'm going. I'm leaving here. I'll go back to them. I don't care what they do to you. I hope they shoot you the minute they see you. Oh, God! I'm so ashamed . . ." Glaring at him, suddenly she screamed, "Get out, will you? Let me get dressed. Take your filthy eyes off me. Get away from me. Get out."

Angry now, Wilder started around the foot of the bed toward her. "Baby, are you a dreamer!" he growled past clenched teeth.

Backing away as he approached, she came in contact with the wall beside the window. Moaning, she recoiled from the wall, her face twisted in pain. "Keep away from me," she panted, sobbing. "Don't touch me. I hate you. Oh, how I hate you. You don't want to love me. I hope they—"

Wilder grabbed for her shoulders.

Cat-quick, she slipped to one side, her face ferocious with hatred, her eyes gleaming now, even when she was no longer in the moonlight.

Circling in front of her, Wilder backed her into a corner, reaching for her once again. He got hold of some of the clothes she held in front of her and pulled her toward him.

One of her hands released its grip on the clothes and snaked out and up, her fingers reaching for his face, curved like claws.

Wilder gasped from the searing wave of pain when her nails raked across his swollen left eye. He ducked his head to one side before she could get another swipe in. One of his hands closed around her wrist in time to keep her from doing any more damage. Swinging his other arm outward, he wrapped it completely around her, pulling her roughly against him, with all her clothing still there, a barrier between their bodies.

He was just beginning to twist the one wrist he had managed to grab, to force her to quit fighting, when she seemed to collapse inward against him, gasping and crying out.

"Please! Don't!" she whimpered. "My back . . ."

"Are you through?" he grunted, glaring down into her face. Her blind eyes stared up at him, unseeing. Her face was contorted with agony. "My back, my back," she groaned. "Please, let go . . ."

He took his arm from around her.

Sighing, she collapsed onto the floor in front of him, landing on top of her clothes. Wilder was so surprised that he released her wrist when her sudden collapse wrenched it out of his hand. Then he noticed her back.

Glorieta had fallen in a heap on the clothes she had been clutching in front of her. The faint moonlight pouring through the window onto her showed the black line of her bra strap and, farther down, the black sheen of her panties.

But that wasn't what made Wilder stare. It was the shape her back was in that caused his voice to die in his throat. He went down on one knee beside her, appalled at what he was seeing.

From the waist all the way up to her shoulder blades, Glorieta's back was a raw mass of dark streaks. There had been some broken skin: narrow patches of scab showed here and there. But mostly it was welts.

In daylight, they would be black and blue, but even in this delusive moonlight, they were ugly looking things to see, ugly even to know about.

Almost tenderly, Wilder asked, "Kiddo, what in the hell happened to your back?" She was sobbing softly, her face pressed into her clothes. "Who did this to you?"

"Tate," she managed to reply through the gasping sobs.

"No wonder you killed the son of a bitch," he murmured. "I don't blame you."

Laughing hysterically, she managed to choke out, "I didn't kill him."

Gently, he put a hand on her head and stroked her hair, feeling the curving fragility of her skull under the sliding mane.

Turning her head, she took hold of his hand with one of hers and pressed his palm against her face. Her cheeks were hot. She kissed his hand.

Lowering himself carefully, Wilder lay on the floor beside her, making certain that he didn't come into contact with her back. Gingerly, he kissed the nape of her neck, pushing her black hair out of the way, holding his lips there a long time, smelling the sweet smell of whatever perfume she wore.

Her crying lessened. She clung to his hand and she still had her face pressed against it while she huskily whispered, "Just love me, Dan. Just make love to me. That's all I want, nothing else. I just want you to come inside me and make me happy. Just do that, Dan. Make love to me, please."

He nodded. "Yeah," he said quietly. He had to clear his throat to get the one word out. His jaws ached from holding his teeth clenched so tightly.

Turning his head, he squinted through the window toward the south, where the other end of Duncan's estate would be.

"I swear I'll kill that old bastard," he muttered. "As sure as morning's on the way, I'll tip that old fart over the edge."

"No, no, darling," she whispered, gazing up at him now. "The poor thing is old, half out of his mind. Don't blame him. He's . . . I guess senile. He's like a cruel child who doesn't know any better. He just stood there, watching it, giggling, while Tate took that big strap to me. He always did that, just stood there, or sat nearby, watching, while one of them gave me a whipping. He'd be drooling and giggling like . . . like something in a zoo. That's really all Jeff is now, Dan. Just an idiot thing inside a body Hendricks and his doctors are keeping alive as long as they can."

Wilder didn't say anything. After watching his face another moment, Glorieta lowered her head into the palm of his hand again.

In a quiet meditative voice, she went on, "Last night was worse than ever before. I was scared, panicky. Tate went out of control. I twisted my head around once . . . he had my wrists tied behind a post . . . and I saw Tate's face and eyes. He looked crazier than my husband." She swallowed and was quiet for a moment before continuing, "When he finally stopped hitting my back with that strap and untied me, I fell to the floor. I was barely conscious. I thought that was the end of it, but . . . it wasn't. Tate turned me over on the floor. He was tearing at his own clothes. He was going to . . ." She stopped speaking and swallowed again, before she could go on. ". . . right there on the floor, in front of Jeff, Tate was going to . . ."

"Quit talking about it," Wilder told her gently. "I can guess the rest."

"I can too," she said, laughing bitterly. "I have to, because I don't know the rest. All I can remember is Tate turning me over onto my back and crashing down on top of me. That's when I passed out. My back was on fire. When he turned me over and the floor touched my back and then he . . . everything disappeared. I blacked out. I never saw Tate again after that last disgusting glimpse I had of him falling on top of me."

"Then your husband must have been the one," Wilder said with conviction. "He must have killed Tate. It had to be either you or Jeff Duncan. Then Hendricks was called in to take care of it and he decided to rig me for the whole thing."

Taking a deep breath, he relaxed a little.

"Okay," he went on, "that'll make it easier, in case I have to start shooting people. I'll make damn sure old Jeff Duncan is one of them. And maybe that Hendricks bastard too, if I can manage it. Yeah, I think I'll make sure of Bert Hendricks, since he's really the one who's been arranging all this business for both of us."

"Dan," she whispered hopelessly, "couldn't we just go away? They'll kill you."

"They'll kill me anyway," he said savagely. "Here or someplace else, same difference. They've stuffed me into the slot there's no statute of limitation on: murder one. Law will always be looking for me, wherever I go. I might as well die here in Thomaston as someplace else."

For a long moment Glorieta didn't say anything, then she murmured, "Danny? We can . . . do it . . . can't we? Even with my back like this? I can be on top. Sometimes it's even better that way . . ."

Wilder began to laugh. With the hand her face was pressed against, he turned her head a bit so he could kiss her lips.

"That's what I've heard tell," he chuckled. "All right, we'll check it out, right now."

She smiled and kissed his lips twice, quickly.

"Yes," she said fiercely, with only a trace of the scratchy sound in her voice again. "Right now, Danny. Help me up, will you darling? Hurry, Dan. Help me over to the bed."

CHAPTER ELEVEN

Wilder came awake, alert and rigid, listening, trying to hear again whatever had reached him in sleep.

No more moonlight came through the south windows of the front room. The night had grown colder too, as if the moon's departure from the night sky had taken all the world's warmth away with it.

Reaching out, Wilder touched one of the guns he had put on a bedside chair. He didn't pick it up, just held his hand on top of it.

Beside him in the bed, Glorieta lay on her stomach. Her breathing was the only thing he could hear but he knew some sound had brought him out of sleep.

The air in the cabin was heavy with dampness from the lake outside, and as cold and dreadful as two o'clock in the morning.

Pulling the rough woolen blanket higher, up to his chin, he went on listening, holding his breath for long stretches. He was still unable to hear anything except the girl's soft regular breathing.

The part of the blanket covering Glorieta had slipped down to her waist. Wilder pulled it higher on her, trying to get it up to her shoulders without hurting her back with it and waking her.

A phone rang in the back room.

Wilder was out of bed and on his feet before the first ring stopped, a gun in each hand.

Glorieta woke, startled. "Dan?" she cried. "What?"

She began to push herself up, but stopped, gasping with the pain her sudden movement brought to her back.

"Where's that phone?" Wilder growled. "Why didn't you tell me there was a phone?"

"The other room," she whispered, turning and getting carefully out of the bed on her side. "To the right as you go in, Dan."

The phone in the back room was on a waist-high shelf in a niche in the wall. Its ringing sounded like a fire alarm bell in the otherwise soundless night.

His back to the wall, Wilder stood beside it, waiting, listening, watching the windows.

It was that little box, he thought, furious. The one he had spotted on top of the gatepost, clicking and buzzing when she used her key.

It might be like that alarm in the finance company heist he had been in on last year, over in St. Louis — the damned alarm went off miles away when a key was inserted and turned. The gatepost box might be wired the same way.

The phone quit ringing, leaving silence like a hole in the night. Wilder stood there in his bare feet, waiting for the ringing to start again, straining to hear it, as if he wanted it to start up again.

Forcing himself to snap out of the trance, he turned irritably and went back into the other room. "Better get dressed," he told Glorieta.

She began asking questions in a whisper, her teeth chattering from the bottom-of-the-night cold, but Wilder didn't bother answering.

Quickly, he got into his clothes and laced his shoes, thinking that every time he went to bed with this woman, they were rousted out of sleep sooner or later by strangers somewhere out there in the night.

When he had his coat on and was slipping the long barrel of the Trooper Colt inside his trouser belt in back, the phone began ringing again.

Going back into the other room, he listened to it, waiting for it to stop. Glorieta came and stood beside him, listening too.

"Should we answer it?" she whispered.

"No. It can only be them — Hendricks or the police. Is this a regular phone? I mean, can we call anywhere?"

"You can get the Thomaston operator."

The ringing stopped, leaving another hole in the dark silence, but not as big as before.

Wilder reached out . . . but his hand hesitated, then withdrew. He gazed down at her pale face. Even in the darkness he could see her glistening eyes.

"I'm going outside," he told her.

"Oh, Dan, don't leave me alone," she protested.

"Don't worry," he assured her. "I've got to take a look around out there. You can do this: stay here by the phone. If you hear me in trouble out there, or any noises, shots, anything at all, dial that operator and holler for Lt. Bricken of the police. If you get through to him, tell him to get out here."

He thought for a moment, then added, "You might not have enough time for all that, so, first thing, you tell the operator who you are and where you are. Then tell her you want Bricken. Got that?"

"Yes."

She hadn't put her shoes on. He could hear her bare feet slapping across the smooth plank flooring of the front room as she walked beside him to the front door.

Before going outside, he stopped and peered down at her white face, a faint pale smudge in the chill cabin's darkness. Putting a hand on her cheek, he ran it around the side of her head and in under her hair.

"Put your coat on," he said quietly. "And your shoes. It's freezing in here. Go on, get your coat on. Then get back to that phone."

"Alright, Dan."

She leaned against him. Her arms went around him under his coat. Her hands flattened against his back inside the slits he had cut in the shirt he'd gotten from Milo.

Her fingers were cold against his skin.

She held on like that a long time. Then she shivered, let go, and went in search of her coat.

When she was putting it on, he could make out the light-colored coat vaguely in the dark room. He heard her slipping into her shoes, and then the pale shape moved across the darkness and vanished into the other room.

Turning, he opened the front door. It creaked as he pulled it inward. Stepping quickly outside, he pulled the door shut behind him. He held the .38 cocked in his right hand down at his side.

Something moved nearby.

Wilder brought the revolver up but he was too slow.

What might have been the barrel of a handgun cracked into his arm inside the bend of the elbow. The blow didn't hurt, but his lower bicep spasmed and the gun went off.

The bullet chunked into the porch flooring. A shriek of pain close by hurt Wilder's ear.

When the shot-flash briefly illuminated the porch, Wilder saw there were two of them, one on each side of the doorway.

"My foot, my foot!" the one on the right was howling. Wilder lashed a quick fist out at that one, but he connected with nothing but air. There was a crashing sound. The one who'd been shot had fallen.

Spinning to his left, Wilder chopped at the other one with a fist sent in around chest high, but it landed against what might have been a shoulder. He shot out a straight punch lower down, trying to get some damage done fast, but no luck, there wasn't any chest there to take the body blow.

The man was still there, however. Wilder could hear him moving close by, so he tried to back away.

The one screaming and hollering on the porch floor behind him was in the way. Wilder stumbled on an arm, the arm rolled beneath his foot, and he lost his balance just when the other one moved in swinging. It was like being slammed in the head with two-thirds of the cabin.

The .38 flew off into the night. Wilder tumbled over backward, clear over the one thrashing in agony on the planks.

Hitting the porch hard on his back, Wilder forced himself to roll and keep rolling until the barky crosspieces of the porch railing brought him up short. Grabbing the railing, he used it to help pull himself to his feet.

Before he was quite upright, the man who had clipped him was on top of him again.

He hooked a fist into Wilder's middle.

Gagging, Wilder doubled over. He could taste some of the water he had drunk earlier.

He was getting groggy. He hardly felt the next blow, a head punch that spun him around so he ended up bent over the porch railing.

Eight feet below, the dark lake water shifted.

"Riker, don't finish him," the one on the floor screeched. "I want that bastard myself. Christ, my foot! I can feel the bone splinters . . ."

Riker chuckled, towering over Wilder.

"Harry, my boy, you can have whatever I leave," he said cheerfully. One of his huge hands grabbed Wilder's shoulder and yanked him off the railing, spinning him around. "Three times you crowbarred me, Wilder!" he was whispering confidentially. "Three across the skull. Wilder-baby, I'm gonna break your bones."

Wilder wrenched his shoulder out of Riker's massive hand, but he still couldn't straighten up from the body blow he had taken.

On the other side of the lodge he heard shouts. One of the back windows was smashed in. Glorieta cried out. Wilder could hear glass splinters falling on the floor inside the cabin.

"Attaboy, Wilder," Riker was chuckling. "Don't fall down. Take it standing. I like a guy who hangs in there and keeps trying." Then he snorted. "No, I don't like that kinda guy at all," he corrected himself genially.

Bent over as he was, Wilder had to look up to see Riker. The big man appeared enormous. He seemed to hang above Wilder like a dark menacing mountain.

Sucking in some careful air, Wilder stabbed his left hand stiff-fingered up toward Riker's diaphragm, but there was neither speed nor power in the thrust.

Riker just grunted, fell back a step, laughed softly, and came on again.

"Thanks, you gun-whipping bastard," he chortled. "It's more fun when you still think you've got some fight left in you."

He slammed a left into Wilder's face.

Wilder bounced off one of the log posts supporting the porch roof. Sliding to his left, he crouched, trying to drive a right upward into Riker's face. He needn't have bothered. It connected, but it only made the big man mad when it scraped along his jaw.

Riker sent a haymaker at him. Wilder sidestepped it.

"Screw this!" Wilder muttered.

He didn't wait for anymore. Turning, he rolled over the porch railing.

As he dropped down into the water he could hear Glorieta screaming inside the cabin. "Danny, help me, help me!" were the last words he heard before he hit the water feet first and went plunging down into the shocking cold. Even at two or three in the morning, no summer lake should have been that cold.

His feet touched bottom but he didn't know which way he was facing, towards shore or away from it. He began swimming underwater anyway, stroking as hard as he could, trying to straighten out a little from the body cramp he'd been in since that first belt in the gut Riker had given him.

The small of his back itched as he swam. Suppose Riker started shooting down into the water? How far down before a bullet going through water won't do any damage?

Wilder had no idea. He had never checked it out.

One of his hands brushed against something. He groped with both hands and found it to be an upright log, one of the posts supporting the porch.

Pulling himself close against its slimy side, he began easing himself upward, guided by the post. His lungs strained for air, but he forced himself to take it slow.

His head broke surface.

He'd been correct; he was under the porch. He'd been swimming toward shore, not away from it.

Just as well; he couldn't have gone far underwater, not with the little bit of air he'd had in his lungs when he'd jumped down from the porch.

Above him, Wilder could just distinguish a vague shape leaning far out, a man peering down at the water.

Footsteps running along one of the side porches sounded like thunder approaching. Another one was coming out of the cabin: Wilder heard the door bang open.

"Riker, she was on the phone," this man yelled. "I stopped her before she got hold of anybody."

The one leaning down turned his head.

"You sure?" Riker asked over his shoulder. He was the one leaning down trying to spot Wilder in the water.

"Positive," the other man said. "The operator was still calling Mrs. Duncan's name, asking what was wrong. I hung up."

Riker pulled back out of Wilder's sight.

"That's not so good," Riker said, "the operator knowing her name. You better give Hendricks a call, up at the main house. Tell him about it. Let him decide what to do about that operator."

Footsteps tattooed rapidly across the porch and on inside the cabin, leaving only the groaning of the one whose foot had been shot.

"And tell Hendricks to send that boat with lights up here," Riker called. "You got the broad secure?"

From inside the cabin, Wilder heard a laugh. "Yeah. I found a pair of handcuffs in here. I put them on her."

Wilder let go of the post he was holding onto with one hand and groped underwater for his coat pocket. The bracelets he had taken from Blubbergut were gone. The key was still there, but no cuffs. Reaching around behind him, he felt for the Trooper in his belt and sighed with relief. He still had that, anyway. He wondered if it would still shoot after this dunking. He would have to clean it when he got out of the lake.

"How's the foot?" he heard Riker ask.

There was no reply from the wounded man, only some muffled cursing. More running footsteps came roaring around the cabin on both side porches.

"Took you long enough," Riker growled at the newcomers.

"You told us to stay put," one of them replied. "You and Harry would yell if you wanted us, you said."

"Okay, okay," Riker replied impatiently. "One of you see how Harry's doing. He caught one in the foot I think. Get him inside."

"Was that the shot we heard?"

"Yeah. Hit his foot or his ankle," Riker said. "Get him inside. He's getting on my nerves. A couple of you guys work along the edge of the lake, both ways. And see if that Wilder bastard is under this porch. The water seems to reach all the way back down there, maybe even partway under the cabin for all I know. I couldn't see him come up, so either he's . . ."

Wilder went below the surface again, pulling himself down the post he'd been clinging to. When he was far enough down, he turned, got his feet under and then behind him, against the slippery post, and propelled himself out into the lake.

Using the breaststroke, he took his time, letting a little air go bubbling out of his mouth with each stroke. When he couldn't hold off any longer, he rolled over onto his back and eased up to the surface. He tried to break surface only with his nose and mouth, but his entire head popped up.

He didn't toss his head to clear his eyes of water. He simply floated there and breathed quietly and took a long careful look back in the direction of the lodge. He could barely make it out in the darkness. Good thing the moon had set. Instead of submerging again, he swam backward on the surface, slowly and carefully, being cautious about the way his feet kicked: he didn't want them to break surface. Splashing sounds would probably carry pretty far on a night this quiet.

The dark outline of the lodge was getting farther off, its shape losing definition as he increased the distance. Now and then, he could still hear voices from back there, but he could no longer make out what they said.

Riker had mentioned a boat with lights. What kind of lights? Wilder tried to get up some speed. He couldn't, not if he kept swimming backward.

For the time being he decided that silence was better than speed. At least he was slowly getting farther away from them.

Wilder wished he had noticed how wide this lake was when the moon had still been out. Turning his head he peered over his shoulder, but the lake's eastern shore was only a black blur below the lesser darkness of the sky.

Shortly afterward lights appeared back by the cabin. Then there were other lights moving along the edge of the lake in both directions near the lodge. Flashlights, probably. Wilder wasn't worried about flashlights: he was far enough away not to be reached by them. Just boats. That was all that was worrying him right now — boats.

He got in another five minutes of swimming before his boat worry became real: he heard a motor approaching from the south.

Wilder looked that way. A long straight finger of light probed far ahead of the swift moving craft.

Rolling over, he began using a long-reaching underwater dog paddle, still making an effort to keep from ruffling surface water with his passage.

His coat dragged. He should probably get rid of it. Same with his shoes. But he couldn't feature running through the woods at night in his bare feet. Or any time, for that matter. The coat, though: he might jettison that.

Giving a quick calculating glance over his shoulder toward the approaching launch, he decided to wait on the coat. Ahead and not too far, the shore he was trying to reach seemed somewhat closer across the dark water. It looked less indistinct than it had up to now.

The approaching boat's powerful engine was getting louder in the night silence. It wasn't long before Wilder could see it wouldn't pass anywhere near him. It was staying close to the west shore of the lake.

Every ten or fifteen strokes, he glanced over his shoulder and took a quick look back that way to keep track of the launch. It slowed and was turning in toward the shore where the lodge should be. Wilder could no longer see the lodge at all. It had merged into the black bulge of land beyond it.

Once when he looked back, he thought he could still glimpse a flash of light from one of the flashlights, but when the boat approached shore and the racket of its motor was cut, its searching beam obliterated any other lights.

Breathing a bubbly sigh of relief, he faced forward once more. Maybe he had a couple of extra minutes.

Ahead, the shore was much nearer now. He could make out the higher land more clearly outlined against the slightly less dark sky framing it.

He was beginning to tire, though. It was taking too long. Quitting the dog paddling below the surface, he began using a crawl stroke. It improved his speed.

Not far to go. Now he could see the shore ahead.

Then, suddenly, he could see it much clearer.

Morning already?

No, it wasn't morning. This sun was coming from the wrong direction to be morning: from behind him.

The shadow of his own head stretched in front of him across the surface of the lake. Wilder whipped his head around. His eyes met the glare of the motorboat's searchlight. It blinded him momentarily.

Facing forward again, he increased the beat of his swimming stroke, feeling rage and helplessness inside, until he realized that they weren't nearly as close upon him as that light of theirs had made him think.

The sound of the motor increased again. It was getting louder a lot quicker than he liked, and the louder it roared, the more frightening it sounded. Underwater again.

Too bad. He could see the shore close ahead, could make out plainly a thick screen of trees and brush coming right down to the water's edge.

Couldn't be helped though, the submerging: if he continued swimming above the surface, they would be on top of him before he could possibly reach shelter among those trees ahead.

Taking a deep breath, Wilder went under, swimming forward and down on a shallow angle, then leveling off. He would have to make it to shallow water on one lungful of air. No breaking the surface and going under a second time.

Knifing his hands forward through the water as far as they would reach, he then swept them wide and brought them around until the palms clapped against his thighs. Then again. And again.

He opened his eyes. It was much brighter underwater than above, but although he ought to be getting close, he couldn't see anything ahead.

He kept on.

His lungs were feeling the strain.

The beat of the approaching launch's engine thudded in his ears.

Not much farther. Another ten strokes? He tried to make it ten. Six. Eight. Only two more.

No good. He couldn't do without air another second. Skyrocket lights were popping in front of his tightly shut eyes now.

Slanting upward, he lunged for the surface and broke through, plunging high out of the water, his mouth wide, gasping, gulping sweet night air into his lungs.

And there in front of him, not ten feet away, the shoreline hovered over the water's edge.

Plopping back down into the water, Wilder drove his arms in strong strokes, hoping to get ashore without being observed by the men in the approaching launch.

Off to his right rear, the speedboat came roaring around in a wide swinging curve. Its powerful light swept along the edge of the lake, picking out thin sapling trees, close together, patches of bushes, naked earth.

Then the beam of light reached Wilder.

He froze in the water. The beam swept past. Exultantly, he swam on. His feet touched bottom. He began to climb, a maddening slow-motion climb, with the water dragging at his straining legs.

The lake bottom rose steeply. He grabbed for branches and then got hold of thin tree trunks to help haul himself up out of the water.

The boat had gone roaring past him, but suddenly, the searchlight swung back. Abruptly, the motor was cut to nothing. "There he is!" someone shouted. "Bring her around."

Wilder plowed upward through clinging mud and crawled over a hump of grass.

"Too late, he's ashore," another voice from the boat said. "Shoot him."

Now that the launch's motor was an almost inaudible rumble, Wilder could hear their voices quite clearly.

"Get in a little closer to shore."

Wilder kept trying to force his way up the steep slope from the water's edge into a thicket of small trees and brush. He couldn't do it; the stuff grew too close together. They were nothing but narrow boles, but there were a lot of them, growing tightly on top of one another. He felt as if he were trying to force himself into a cage.

His back was crawling, waiting for their bullets.

Giving it one last try, he threw himself against the resilient wall of bushes and trees. When they repelled him once again, he gave it up, pulled himself out from the edge of the tangle and yanked the Trooper Colt from under his belt in back. Turning, he raised it, sighted at the searchlight, and pulled the trigger.

Nothing but a click!

Cursing, Wilder dove down into the mud, just as they fired. He didn't care how many shots they got off. All he cared about was that none of them had hit him. Yet.

Scrambling furiously to his knees, he plunged through the muck at the lakeside, parallel to shore, grabbing with his left hand for anything he could reach on the steep bank: bushes, thin tree trunks, anything.

Half in the water, half out of it, he kept going like that.

The men in the launch were still taking potshots at him. Their slugs whipped nearby branches and leaves, plunked soggily into the mud, spat into drier ground farther upslope.

Off to Wilder's right, water leaped, spraying droplets up into his face. Instinctively, he brought his right arm up, as if that would protect him from a bullet, if one connected.

His right hand still held the Trooper. It was no help to him anymore, so he jammed it back under his belt, but in front this time.

After a hard fall among rocks, he regained his footing and slogged on along the edge of the lake, stumbling through the clinging mud as well as he could, trying to spot a break in the veritable wall of thick undergrowth choking the steep slope just above the mud line.

By now, his pursuers had gotten the launch turned and it was coming back in toward shore. They had quit shooting. When they were close enough, they would probably begin again. Wilder had the feeling that this time they wouldn't miss.

Then he fell into a ditch.

Cursing steadily, he got up off his face, and then suddenly he stopped cursing. His hands were touching rocks, not mud. Small rocks.

He had stumbled into a stream bed. Peering upward to his left, he saw the gap in the undergrowth. Getting off his hands and knees, he plunged toward the opening.

Tree roots tripped him, branches grabbed at his clothes, but he ignored all of it, ducking lower to avoid the obstacles and climbing on, sloshing through water up to his knees at first, then only ankle-deep, and finally he was on dry land.

He clambered on up the feeder stream's gully toward the top of the ridge.

Behind him, the men in the launch were yelling to each other. They fired shots again, but mostly it was yelling now.

Wilder didn't slow down, though. Bullets might still bring him down with nothing but bushes and tree leaves to deflect them. He didn't allow himself to stop until he finally crested the ridge and plunged with relief a dozen steps down the far side.

Then at last he started looking around.

There was little to see. He was surrounded by thick undergrowth. Every leaf he brushed against sent a shower of night-moisture down on him.

His coat sleeve snagged on a branch. Taking his time, he stopped and worked it free without ripping the material more than it was torn already.

Farther downslope, the brush began to thin somewhat. He could straighten from the bent over way he had been forced to move. The trees didn't grow so close to one another now.

Wilder just hoped he was still headed away from the lake. Ahead, another hill rose against the sky. He climbed it through thinning woods, going straight up, went over the crown and down the other side.

More hills were beyond that one, two or three more.

Then, down through trees from the top of one of the highest hills he had yet encountered, he saw a faint gleam in the darkness ahead.

Working his way down to it, he ran into a wire fence, got through it between strands a foot apart without ripping his clothes, and climbed up onto an asphalted road.

Without pausing, he turned right onto it at a run, taking it easy, but staying at it as long as he possibly could. He hoped the road would take him to the southern end of the lake and maybe even to the main house Glorieta had talked about.

When he was winded and had to let the running go for awhile, he slowed to a walk until he got his breath back.

Once his breathing was fairly even, he started running again.

Wilder didn't know how far he had to go before he reached the vicinity of old Jeff Duncan's main house at the other end of the estate, but he knew that if he didn't get there before the sun rose, he probably wasn't going to get there at all.

Now he regretted telling Glorieta to phone that cop, Bricken.

One of Riker's buddies had prevented her from completing the phone call she'd tried to make, but Wilder knew that even if she had only been able to tell the operator the one word, police, it might have been enough. The cops would have come swarming out this way in double-time.

They were probably out this way already.

CHAPTER TWELVE

They were. An hour later, Wilder spotted a patrol car an eighth of a mile ahead on the road. He'd have to go back into the woods to get past it.

Turning off, he went a little way in among the trees and suddenly he came in sight of the lake again. Across the stretch of water, all lit up at the top of a vast sweep of what was probably a lawn bigger than most golf courses, stood an enormous mansion with dozens of its windows lighted. Wilder didn't waste time admiring it, but pressed on through the trees until he was close to the water's edge. Apparently the lake had swung closer to the roadway at this southern end.

A little farther along on his left, the lake ended. A private bridge spanned a stream that emptied the lake water after it spilled over a concrete dam.

Now Wilder took a moment to study the big house. It veritably blazed with lights, mostly on the ground floor. It had to be Duncan's joint. His would be the only place around with any reason to turn on that many lights at four or five in the morning.

Turning, Wilder kept going parallel to the shore, keeping back among the trees. When he was almost to the dam, the trees thinned and he could see the police car once more, parked athwart the road at the eastern entrance to the bridge. Its position was such that it commanded a view both of the road Wilder had been traveling along and of the road across the bridge spanning the outlet stream beyond the dam.

As Wilder watched, another car approached from the south and stopped when the cop flagged it down. He must have recognized whomever it was, because he waved it on after only a brief glance.

The car drove across the little bridge, following its own headlights among a belt of trees on the other side. Emerging into the open on the trees' far side, it drove diagonally across the vast gently sloping hillside to the mansion outlined darkly against the western sky.

Leaving the concealment provided by the trees, Wilder went down closer to the lakeshore and worked his way along it to the dam.

The top of the concrete spillway was about as wide as an ordinary sidewalk on a neighborhood street.

Before going near it, Wilder checked the patrol car. An open field separated him from the county road, but if the cop glanced toward the dam, he would probably be able to spot anyone trying to cross on it. Then, too, there was always that searchlight their patrol cars were equipped with. If the cop inside got even a little curious, all he had to do was throw the beam over this way, and it was good-bye Wilder. There would be no contest.

He slipped back into the woods while he thought the odds through, pondering the possibility of trying the bridge the car had just driven across. He decided not to: that was even closer to the patrol car than the dam.

Off in the east behind him, a thin line of light traced the edge of the world. A dog *hoof-hoofed* in the distance.

It would have to be the dam.

Leaving the cover of the trees once again, Wilder started across the dam, walking upright. The water slipping over the top of the spillway tugged at his ankles, but by bracing each foot firmly upon setting it down, he decided he ought to be alright.

Halfway across to the far side, the scum on the concrete made it slippery underfoot. A couple of times Wilder nearly slipped and fell. After it happened once too often, he decided not to chance staying upright any longer, and went down on his hands and knees.

His wet clothes still hung heavily on him from his swim across the upper end of the lake. Now in an instant, the trouser legs were drenched again. Even his coat sleeves sopped up water halfway to his elbows.

Crawling almost seemed to be worse than walking upright. The slithering water had that much more of him to push against. However, there was one advantage: his right hand could grasp the upstream edge of the dam on the lakeside. Moving his hand forward with his fingers curled and gripping the edge, he clung tightly, and he safely went the remaining distance across.

A moment after reaching the far side of the dam, he slipped into the welcoming darkness of the belt of trees.

Peering back across the tumbling stream sluicing in its streambed below the foot of the concrete spillway, he saw the cop still sitting inside his squad car, keeping the roadblock in operation. So he hadn't noticed a thing.

Wilder found a twig and then tore off part of Milo's shirttail. The cloth was still heavy with dampness from the swim across the lake, but Wilder didn't need it completely dry for what he was going to use it on.

Snapping the cylinder out of the Trooper, he ejected the bullets, wiped them with the bit of cloth, and stowed all of them in a pocket of his suit coat. Then, with the cloth wrapped around the twig, he began cleaning and hopefully even drying the cylinder, the chamber, and finally inside the barrel itself.

There turned out to be some guck inside the barrel. He was probably lucky it hadn't fired when he'd pulled the trigger at the other end of the lake. It might have backfired from the mud in the barrel and blown his hand off.

When he had the Trooper as clean and dry as he was going to get it, he reloaded the weapon and carried it in his hand as he went through the rest of the narrow stretch of woods and started across the open land, up toward the big mansion that seemed to dominate everything in sight.

Maybe the Trooper wouldn't work. Maybe all the bullets were ruined from the water. Then again, maybe not. He'd have to chance it.

Wilder approached the Duncan mansion on the run. The closer he got to it, the higher the building seemed to rise above him.

It took him a long time to get near it too. From the other side of the lake, it hadn't appeared too far off, but after crossing the driveway the car had used and running on a slant up the gentle rise, Wilder realized the mansion had seemed to be nearer than it was because of its incredible size.

He still hadn't reached some flower gardens near the south end of the building when the first tentative rays of the morning sun touched some of the turrets and gables up on the roof.

On close inspection, the structure was unbelievable. Architecturally, it had been done in Indianapolis monstrous.

Halting when he came to the flowerbeds, Wilder crouched for a moment's breather, after the long trot up the gentle slope. He used the time to stare up at the house.

It looked like a museum a madman might have had built during a six month drunk. Then Wilder began examining more closely the side of the house directly in front of him.

Lights shone from many of the windows on the ground floor and from a few on the second floor. At the far end of the garden where he crouched, a terrace of some kind projected out from the main floor a step or two above ground level.

Around in back were what looked like smaller buildings, maybe garages. No lights were on in any of those, so he ignored them and concentrated on the lighted windows, especially the ones on the ground floor.

He couldn't see anyone moving around inside any of those lit-up rooms, so he checked behind him to make certain no cars were coming up the long drive angling across the sloping lawn from the bridge. With the coast clear for the moment, he rose and skirted the flower beds, heading for the terrace.

Mounting several flagstone steps, he approached a row of French doors and tried the handles. None would open. He tried to see if anyone was inside but couldn't.

Wilder was about to put an elbow through one of the panes of glass when lights went on inside.

Spinning away, he silently faded along the side of house, getting out of reach of the unexpected illumination. Once he was off the terrace's flagstones, he sheltered among a string of blue spruce trees growing close to the side of the house.

When he thought he was far enough away from the terrace, he squatted and watched the lighted French doors. He waited to see if the lights inside the terrace room stayed on. If they did, he would have to get around to the back and try to gain entry there. With the sun about to come up behind him, he couldn't stay on this side of the house. He was too exposed, spruce trees or no spruce trees.

One of the French doors opened. A man stepped out onto the flagstones. It was Riker. He stood gazing off at the eastern horizon, watching the sun peep over the edge of the world.

Wilder didn't budge. He hardly dared to breathe.

Riker seemed to be looking directly at him, hunched down there behind one of the trees. A voice from inside called, "Riker?"

Riker turned his head slightly. "Out here," his heavy voice rumbled.

The man who emerged onto the terrace wasn't as big as Riker across the shoulders, but he only needed an inch or two in height.

Crossing the terrace, he stood beside Riker, talking quietly to him. Wilder couldn't hear what was said.

He inspected the newcomer: dark-haired but looked over fifty, so Wilder assumed the hair wasn't really dark.

This might be Hendricks.

Thinking that, Wilder gave the man a closer look.

Yes, he had seen this one the night before, coming out of the building Hendricks lived in, down there in Thomaston. Riker had held the car door for him.

So this was The Man, Hendricks the operator, the one who ran things.

Cautiously, Wilder moved forward toward the terrace, staying close to the side of the building and always making sure one or more of the short thick blue spruces was between himself and the two men on the terrace.

Both of them were facing the other way now, but Wilder still moved carefully. Any sound he made would have them looking in his direction in nothing flat.

He was almost to the terrace, with only one of the little spruce trees left as concealment, before he could hear anything the two men were saying.

Hendricks had been speaking vehemently, but too low for Wilder to understand any of it. Then Hendricks quit talking and just stared across the sweep of lawn and the distant belt of trees at the southern end of the lake and the low hills beyond.

Presently, without looking at Riker, Hendricks said, "We've got to get hold of Wilder before Bricken does. We have to silence Wilder. We've got to."

"That's past," Riker said, glancing at the other man. "Stop fretting about it. The cops'll get him. They may even have caught him already."

"No," the other man said, shaking his head. "I mean we've got to get him—"

"I know what you mean," Riker replied irritably.

Ignoring the interruption, the other man went on, "It's dragged on too long. My God, yesterday it could have been so simple. But the longer Wilder is on the loose, the more time Bricken has to wonder. And the more sweating that Morey does."

Patiently, Riker tried to reassure him. "Bert, we can't do anything more, not now. A few of the boys are still up at the lodge, nosing around, but once Wilder swam across the lake, it was pretty much out of our hands. We can't keep the troopers from looking around here. This isn't Thomaston. And you may have noticed that some of the men Bricken brought along are his picked men, the ones we haven't gotten to yet."

Hendricks looked more dissatisfied than ever but he made no reply.

"And don't worry about Wilder getting away," Riker added. "We'd be nuts to interfere now. Sure, I'd like to gun the bastard down myself, for what he did to Redding and for those dents he put in the back of my skull, but . . . let's face it: we're too late. Leave him to Bricken's cops."

Wilder hefted the Trooper Colt he held in his hand. He wished he could be sure of the bullets in the damn thing. Right now he felt like burning down the two of them, right where they stood.

Getting a grip on himself, he shook his head. Better not even try. Maybe it was just as well he had gotten the gun wet, if that was all he had on his mind — shooting people. Killing these two creeps wouldn't help him at all. He had to find another way out of this bind he was in.

Hendricks was staring moodily down at the terrace flagstones when the top edge of the sun popped suddenly above the eastern horizon. Hendricks raised his head, squinted at the unexpected dazzling light, then turned his back to it and looked up at Riker.

"I suppose you're right," he murmured. "Too bad. I suppose something like this was bound to happen, sooner or later. Some character like Wilder was almost certain to come along and mess with Glorieta . . . with Mrs. Duncan. And he wouldn't sit still afterward for your people to get their exercise." He sighed. "I've always known it was going to blow up, eventually, but I didn't think, when it did, it would be this public. If only Tate hadn't tried—"

Riker glanced curiously at the older man. "Tried what?"

"Nothing." Hendricks shook his head impatiently.

Riker shrugged. "Okay, forget Tate. Think of the—"

"How can I forget Tate?" Hendricks protested. "Bricken isn't forgetting him. And Morey's getting the sweats. He's starting to worry. I can tell by that look on his moon face."

"Forget both of them," Riker said calmly. "Leave Morey to me. If he begins to come apart at the seams, I'll give him a taste of the fear of God like he's never had it before."

"No, Riker," objected Hendricks placatingly. "Don't pull any rough stuff on Morey. One dead cop is enough. Too much, in fact. We can handle this but let's do it carefully."

Turning, Hendricks took a quick glance at the climbing sun and hastily turned away again from the brightness of the level rays.

"If only this had held off for one more year," he muttered with exasperation. "Even six months would have been enough time. But I can't let anything happen to that old slob yet, not this close to the whole pile of it. Just a little more time should do it. We'll have complete control and we'll be rolling in the stuff."

With sudden urgency Hendricks headed for the French door. In the doorway he glanced back at Riker. "I'll keep you posted."

"About what?"

"About Wilder, when they find him."

"Oh." Riker shrugged. "Yeah, do that. Bricken still here?"

"Yes. He's inside, trying to get hold of Les Perkins, to see if he has spare keys for those handcuffs one of your bright boys snapped onto Glorieta's wrists last night."

"For Christ's sake, can't anyone pick a lock anymore?" Riker laughed.

"And that's another thing," Hendricks cried angrily. "Why did the damn fool have to put those bracelets on the poor girl. Where the devil did he think she was going? Didn't it occur to the idiot that Wilder would still have those keys on him? How did he think we'd get the goddamn things off?"

Riker chuckled. "Simmer down, Bert," he advised. "Relax. We can always hacksaw them off. Settle down. You're getting edgy. In two more hours they'll haul Wilder in, and then all this will calm down again, and it will all be just the way it was. Maybe better. After this, maybe Mrs. Duncan won't be getting any more of those ideas of hers. After all this ruckus, maybe little Glorieta will be a helluva lot easier to handle . . ."

Hendricks stared at the big man a moment with anger in his eyes. "I hope so," he muttered. But he didn't sound too convinced. Without another word, he disappeared inside.

Riker remained on the terrace another moment, gazing after the departed man.

From inside the room came the sound of a door opening and closing.

Turning to watch the morning sun, Riker's huge shoulders rose and widened as he took a deep breath. Stretching his arms out to each side, he yawned prodigiously. Then, shaking his head and chuckling, he went inside too.

Wilder gave it a minute after the French door closed.

When he thought he had given Riker enough time to get beyond hearing distance of the French doors, Wilder emerged from behind the nearest spruce tree and crossed the terrace to the door Riker had just shut. He tried it. It wouldn't open, so he hammered the butt of the Trooper through one of the panes of glass, reached through the new opening and turned the door handle inside. Someone would spot the fragments of glass on the flagstones out here and the carpet inside, but not for awhile.

The room he entered was unoccupied. Crossing it, he opened a door and slipped through into an enormous corridor, still gloomy and dark, maybe always gloomy and dark.

Glancing both ways along it, he saw no one and started toward the front of the house.

Thick carpeting was underfoot and he could hear the subdued sound of voices somewhere ahead.

The long hall's gloom was broken by a light coming from a half-open doorway. That seemed to be where the voices came from.

Easing past the foot of a wide carpeted staircase, Wilder got over to the wall on that side of the corridor, trying to get near enough to hear what those voices were saying, and if possible to learn who owned the voices.

He didn't like the idea of hunting for old Jeff Duncan in this museum without first getting that cop, Bricken, well bracketed.

A faint moan drifted from somewhere behind Wilder.

For a second, he froze, then spun around, holding the Trooper Colt ready, wishing he could be sure of the bullets it held.

He couldn't see anyone in the high-ceilinged hallway. Night-darkness still filled its entire length.

Again he heard the moaning sound. His skin crawled.

Taking a deep shaky breath, Wilder stepped out into the middle of the hall, gripping the Trooper tightly. He could feel a touch of panic getting to him. He had to hold onto himself hard to keep from letting any of the panic gum things up. He had traveled too long and hard a road to blow the whole thing just because of some creepy haunted house groans.

A third time he heard the sound. He looked upward.

At the top of the staircase, a figure in white stood with a bent head surrounded by wild white hair, peering down at him almost shyly. A shaft of sunlight just beyond the figure made the white hair glow like a nimbus.

Deep in his throat, Wilder growled, but he didn't know he was growling. It came from a lot farther back than the stone age.

Raising the gun, he was about to flip the hammer back when he realized that the figure up there was nothing more terrifying than an old man dressed in some sort of night-gown or hospital tunic, the kind they make invalids wear.

A long shuddering breath escaped Wilder's lips. Grinning sheepishly at his terror a moment ago, he lowered the gun.

He was about to start up the stairs when he remembered the voices behind him, emanating from a room near the front end of the hall. Casting a quick glance that way, he made sure no one had come out into the hall to investigate the creepy sound effects a few moments before.

No one had. Maybe the moaning sounds hadn't carried that far. Reassured, Wilder eased on up the stairs, staying close to the wall.

The white garbed figure shuffled off a short distance as Wilder approached the top. When he started toward it, the man turned away and began a kind of aimless scuttling to the back of the house.

"Wait," Wilder called softly.

The pathetic man looked fearfully over his shoulder. Skin hung from the bones of his face, wrinkled and loose, as if it covered a face that had once had much bigger muscles before age had shrunk them.

Because of the old man's fright, the face looked almost grotesquely funny. Terror bulged his eyes.

"Wait," Wilder called again. "It's alright."

Catching up to the old man, he took hold of one of the pitifully thin arms. The creature stopped and huddled against the wall. Wilder could feel thin muscles and the old arm bone between his gripping fingers, through a rough cotton sleeve.

The terrified eyes stared up at him. The mouth hung open, slack and perpetually moving, dripping saliva. The old head shook on a sadly inadequate neck.

"Don't . . . don't . . ." a remnant of a voice whispered.

So this is Jeff Duncan, Wilder thought. *The terror of Thomaston and environs!*

"Old man," Wilder asked quietly. "Listen, old man. You're Jeff Duncan?"

Sounds came from the mouth but none made sense.

It was Duncan, though. It couldn't be anyone else.

Wilder stared down into the crazy frightened eyes, repelled by the way the old face was constantly working, shaking its wrinkled dangling jowls.

Sighing, Wilder shook his head. This was just something old and sick, something that should have been allowed to die long ago.

"No, old man," Wilder murmured aloud. "I can't kill you."

He released his grip on the rickety arm.

"You're not Jeff Duncan anymore. You're not anyone, really, not anymore."

When Wilder released him, the old man turned and shuffled a few feet along the wall and stood leaning against it, bent a bit, watching Wilder turn and start over toward the head of the stairs.

He had reached the top step and was about to start down when a sharp cry halted him.

"Way-y-y!"

Startled by the urgency in the voice, Wilder halted and glanced back. The old man was still using the wall to prop himself up, but now he stood straighter, taller. One of his hands was extended toward Wilder palm-up, like a beggar.

"Way-y-y!" the wet lolloping lips called again.

Wilder's jaws tightened. It gave him the shivers, just being this close to a half-dead man.

Turning, he started down the stairs again, but something about the old creature now made him pause and take a second look.

He couldn't identify what it was about the old man that had changed, but something had.

Shrugging, he went back over to the figure leaning against the wall, and gazed into the old man's eyes. They stared out at him as if they were inside two caves, but . . . now they seemed somehow to be the eyes of a sane creature.

Perhaps the remnants of control left in the old guy's brain were momentarily fighting a successful skirmish against the encroaching waves of destruction which tissue breakdown within was remorselessly engulfing him.

"Can you . . .?" The merest whisper, like a gentle breeze in the morning quiet. "Could you . . .?" The voice faltered again. The old man gasped under the strain of trying to speak. These weren't the babbling sounds Wilder had heard earlier. Suddenly, clearly, the voice whispered, "Could you . . . give me something?"

Delicately, the voice pushed the words into the cool close gloom of the upper hallway. The fine white hair fluffed out around the bony skull. Each separate strand seemed to catch and retain its own fragile light.

"Could you . . . put me . . . to sleep?" the whisper asked.

Then Wilder understood. "Kill you? Is that what you want?"

From half a world, half a lifetime away, "Ess-s-s-s!" a soft sibilant hopeless sound, sighing into the enormous silence of the morning.

Uncertainly, Wilder hefted the Trooper Colt in his hand.

He gazed at the bony skull with the almost transparent wrinkled skin dangling loosely around it, and at the suddenly clear eyes burning into his own. The eyes bulged and strained to see him as if they were fighting something, perhaps their own damaged vision.

Then the eyes wavered, seemed to stray, as if the mind controlling them was relaxing its delicately maintained tension, allowing them to slip away from his face and wander. But each time this happened, or began to happen, the eyes would swing back to Wilder's face, would become sharply focused again, would see Wilder again, would continue their struggle to go on seeing him, only to begin straying once more, rolling vacantly away.

Wilder half-raised the Trooper, seemed to be straining mightily to lift it the rest of the way. Then he let it fall to his side again, shaking his head in defeat.

"I can't," he almost snarled. "Listen, old man, I can't. I'd be killing myself too."

He flung his gun arm out, pointing the muzzle of the weapon down the staircase.

"They don't understand these things," he said, speaking in a gentler voice. "They make laws . . ."

"Pluh . . . pleeeeze!" the wet quivering lips gasped, softly. "I was . . . a man. Now . . . a thing. Don't . . . let me go . . . back."

The bulging eyes closed. The head tilted a bit on the too thin neck, only to tilt upright again when the eyes sprang open, wild, desperately fighting a hopeless struggle to hold onto the moment of lucidity, trying to keep it from being swamped.

"Couldn't you . . . give . . . something . . . put me to . . . sleep? . . . I won't tell . . ."

Wilder couldn't take any more. Turning away, he plunged down the stairs.

Behind him, the thin voice rose in an agonized shriek, "Oh, ple-e-e-ease!"

The sound of the forlorn cry seemed to swell and grow in volume in the echoing hallway of the enormous building. Wilder didn't pause in his descent, but the farther down the stairs he went, the louder that long cry of sorrow seemed to become.

Up toward the front of the main floor's corridor, two men emerged from the room where the light came from. Both were staring back toward the stairs.

Turning at the foot of the staircase, Wilder ran back the way he'd come earlier. He couldn't tell now which door led to the room with the French doors.

Ahead of him, toward the back of the hallway, another door burst open, admitting a nurse in a white uniform into the corridor. From still another room, farther back, three men joined her.

Wilder quit running and looked over his shoulder toward the front. Three of them were coming from there, running.

Turning to the nearest door, Wilder tried to open it and found it locked. He ran to the next door and found that one locked too.

Riker's voice was booming beyond the approaching men, "It's Wilder. He's carrying a gun. Shoot him."

Someone fired.

Wilder hit the carpet, swiveled around to face the nearing three, sighted the Trooper on the closest one, and squeezed off.

Nothing.

He pulled the trigger again and again. Still nothing.

Now they were firing from both ends of the hallway. One slug shot into the thick carpet close to his head. He flinched away from it, snapping his eyes shut.

Racing through his mind was the thought that they would be knocking each other off, if they kept on shooting both ways.

He hoped they did.

Although it was useless, he kept pulling the trigger. Still the Trooper Colt didn't fire. He wondered how long that Blubbergut had kept those bullets in his big handgun. It was either that or all of them had been ruined by that goddamn swim across the lake.

They were getting close now, still firing wildly.

Someone up front beyond Riker was yelling in a huge voice, "Stop firing, Riker. Cease fire, all of you."

Wilder paid no attention to that. Riker was the kind of bastard who would stop when he was good and ready to stop, not before.

Taking a deep breath that seemed to go on and on, he drew air into his starving lungs. Then, clenching his teeth, he pushed himself up from the warm protection of the carpet and came lunging to his feet.

Wilder threw the Trooper at the man nearest him, saw him double over when the big revolver thudded into his middle, and felt the heat of the muzzle blast when the gun he held fired into the wall. Then he went down and Wilder was leaping over the sprawling form, headed for the next one behind him.

That one was squeezing off his shots too fast. One of the slugs whipped by, too close, and then Wilder was into him, swinging with both fists.

That one went down.

Wilder tripped over him, half-sprawling beyond him, somehow recovered his footing and went racing on, bulling into the next one.

But that one was Riker.

There was no pile driving over someone as big as Riker.

Wilder managed to get in two good swings when they collided, but Riker just hooked one arm around Wilder, dragged him to the floor and got on top of him when he went down.

Wilder clamped both hands onto Riker's gun arm, but that was about all he could manage. He knew he couldn't hold Riker's arm with only one hand while he used the other to try taking the gun away from him.

He could feel the overwhelming strength surging in Riker's arm as it resisted the grip of both Wilder's hands.

Then it was over.

The yelling and shooting suddenly subsided. Lights were turned on along the corridor.

Directly above his head, a calm voice said, "That's enough, Mr. Wilder. It's been a long twenty-four hours, but now it's over."

Wilder was looking up at a hard muscled face with steady gray eyes and a touch of gray in a full head of hair.

"Get up from there, both of you," he ordered.

Carefully, Wilder struggled to his feet, hanging onto Riker's gun arm until he felt Riker relax and start to put the gun away.

"You're Lt. Bricken?" Wilder asked, still watching Riker.

"Yes, I'm Bricken." The steady eyes rested on Wilder for a moment. Then Bricken turned away and called, "Sgt. Morey, take this man into the front room. I'll be right with you."

"Better remind Morey not to shoot me in the back on the way," Wilder suggested. Laughing, he added, "For trying to escape, of course."

Bricken frowned at Wilder and jerked his head peremptorily toward the front of the house.

"Go on," he told Morey. "I'll be along in a minute."

As Morey herded Wilder along, the sergeant smirked. "You coulda saved all of us a lot of work, toughie," he muttered sourly.

"You afraid of honest work, Morey?" Wilder asked.

"Where'd it all get you?" Morey jeered. Coming along close behind Wilder, he reached out and shoved Wilder, pushing him along the corridor. "Keep moving, toughie."

Wilder stopped and turned to face him.

"Hands off," he growled.

Morey chuckled and gave him another shove. Wilder leaned into it and didn't budge. Lifting his service revolver, Morey waved it menacingly under Wilder's nose. He was grinning, but he looked a bit uneasy too.

"Don't give me no trouble, toughie."

"You lay another hand on me," Wilder said evenly, "and I'll make you use that gun. You think Bricken will like that? You think nothing about you smells yet?"

Morey tried to look threatening, but he couldn't quite bring it off. "Come on," he snarled half-heartedly. "Move the lard. The lieutenant wants you in the front room, so get going."

Wilder nodded, turned, and went along the corridor to the door with the light shining out.

Inside, Morey instructed him which chair to sit on, by the wall opposite the doorway.

Only when Wilder was seated did he notice Glorieta Duncan lying fast asleep, facedown, on a leather covered divan over in the corner on his right.

CHAPTER THIRTEEN

When Bricken finally came in from the hall, he was followed by Riker and two uniformed police officers. One of them was saying, "Lieutenant, I can't get hold of that Perkins fellow out at the county jail."

A white uniformed nurse followed them in and went directly over to Glorieta.

Bricken nodded acknowledgement of what he'd been told, but he only appeared irritated by it. Shaking his head, he thought of something, and glanced across at Wilder.

"Do you have a key to those confounded handcuffs, Mr. Wilder?"

"What handcuffs?"

"The ones you stole from Les Perkins yesterday morning, when you racked up his car south of town."

"Oh, yeah," Wilder said. "In my pocket here."

"I'll get them," Bricken told him sharply, coming over. "Stand up."

Wilder rose, Bricken got the key, frisked Wilder thoroughly almost as an afterthought, then went over to take the cuffs off Glorieta's wrists.

"Can I go now?" Wilder asked.

Bricken ignored him. Slipping the cuffs into a pocket, he sighed, "Now perhaps we can get around to the unimportant things."

He faced Riker, but before he could speak, Hendricks entered from the corridor. Bricken glanced at the new arrival, but returned his attention to Riker.

"Why all that shooting awhile ago, Mr. Riker?" he demanded. "Since when do you and all those people of yours pack iron?"

"Just being careful, Lieutenant," replied Riker. "We heard that Wilder had Les Perkins's gun, so, since we were helping your police in the search for him up at the other end of the lake, I thought we should be carrying heat of our own."

Obviously, Bricken wasn't satisfied by the explanation, but after a moment, he grudgingly nodded. "I'll accept part of that," he said, "but there is no excuse for blasting away whenever you feel like it. This man didn't fire a single shot out in that corridor, yet everyone was firing away like it was target time at the county fair. It's a miracle no one was hit. Thank God you're all such lousy shots."

"I wasn't one of the ones shooting or he would have been hit," Riker said. His face looked tough and stubborn for a moment, but then he made it relax. "Okay, you're probably right, Lieutenant. Sorry. The boys should have held their fire."

Bricken was somewhat mollified by Riker's attitude.

"All right," he said after a moment. Turning his attention from Riker, he said, "Mr. Hendricks, we'll be out of here in two shakes now that Wilder is in custody."

"Fine, fine, Lieutenant," Hendricks said gratefully. "Just let me know if there's anything I can do. Glad to help, anytime."

"I'll want Mrs. Duncan available for the preliminary hearing, for one thing," Bricken replied. "I would appreciate your seeing that she's available."

"Certainly," Hendricks said smoothly. "Of course, that will depend on Mrs. Duncan's physical condition. As a result of . . ." his glance flickered toward Wilder ". . . the recent disturbances, what with Mrs. Duncan being dragged off to the upper end of the lake by this murdering . . . well, all of it has left the poor woman in a state bordering on shock. She is an extremely sensitive woman, Lieutenant. You understand. Her availability for questioning in connection with all this will depend on whatever her physician considers advisable."

"She seemed all right to me when I spoke to her earlier," Bricken broke in impatiently, glancing over at Glorieta, still lying asleep, facedown on the divan. "Maybe a bit tired . . ."

The nurse hovering near Glorieta spoke up. "I administered a mild sedative to Mrs. Duncan, Lieutenant. I didn't know you needed her testimony this morning."

"We don't," Bricken replied testily, "not right this morning." He shrugged. "Okay, I'll have a word with her doctor about it later."

"Shall I get the doctor now?" the nurse asked. "I think he's upstairs with poor Mr. Duncan."

"Yes, would you?" Bricken said absently. "Whenever he can get down here."

The woman left on soundless rubber soled feet. Hendricks had drifted over to stand beside the divan, gazing down at Glorieta.

Wilder watched him a moment, then noticed Riker eyeing Hendricks, too, with just a trace of a sardonic smile on his wide brutal mouth.

Frowning, Wilder spoke on impulse. "Lieutenant, I'd feel a lot better if you got some answers from Mrs. Duncan before we leave this room."

"You would, would you?"

Bricken didn't even glance in Wilder's direction.

"Yes, I would. I get this feeling she won't be available for questioning after today. Her doctor is almost certainly going to advise against her being disturbed, ever."

Hendricks turned from contemplating Glorieta and stared across the room at Wilder.

Now Bricken looked at Wilder.

"What has Mrs. Duncan got to do with any of this, Mr. Wilder?" the detective asked. "You're wanted for questioning in the murder of Ofc. Tate."

"Who accuses me?" Wilder shot back. "Morey?"

Bricken turned away contemptuously without replying.

"Lieutenant, I didn't kill Tate."

Bricken smiled, nodding wearily. "You'll have ample opportunity to present your side of the case, Mr. Wilder. I don't know a thing about it. I wasn't even assigned the Tate case, only this part of the search for you. So there's no use in your trying to get me to—"

"There's no use and no hope for me at all if you leave here without getting some answers from Mrs. Duncan. Morey is lying if he testified that I could have killed Tate."

Bricken spun around. His eyes flashed angrily. He advanced toward Wilder. His hands had become fists swinging heavily at his sides.

But before he reached Wilder, Bricken made himself stop, with obvious difficulty. He was shaking with his sudden anger.

"You cheap grifter," he whispered. "Don't say a word to me about any officer in my department. I've heard it all, too many times. We're framing you, are we? You won't get an honest trial, will you? Sgt. Morey is jeopardizing his career on the force by giving false testimony, is he? Someone else killed Tate, not you. Is that the way you're telling it?"

Quietly Wilder said, "That's exactly the way I'm telling it, Lieutenant."

His mouth ugly with disdain, Bricken shook his head. "You slobs never change, do you?"

"Neither do self-righteous cops like you," Wilder replied hotly. "Or the ones on the take, like Morey, the ones who are always on the take—"

Turning to Morey, Bricken jerked an impatient thumb at Wilder. "Get him out of here, Sergeant."

"My pleasure, sir," Morey said emphatically.

Wilder chuckled. "You want to bet I don't get shot in the back before Morey gets me to your town pokey, Lieutenant?"

Bricken ignored him.

Wilder rose and faced Morey, backing away from him until the wall behind him brought his retreat to a stop.

Taking out his service revolver, Morey told him, "Now don't give me no more hard time, you. This time you ain't about to throw any chairs at me."

"Use the gun now, Morey," Wilder told him. "You might as well." Glancing down at the wreck his suit had become, he grinned slightly.

"I don't want my clothes getting all dirtied up in whatever ditch you dump me in on your way into town."

Bricken turned and stared intently at him.

"You're really serious, aren't you?" he asked incredulously. "You actually believe—"

"Ask Glorieta Duncan," Wilder interrupted him. "Tate took her with him and left me and Morey in my motel room."

"I told you before!" Bricken shouted furiously. "It isn't my case. I don't know anything about any of it."

"Then find out about it!" Wilder shouted back. "If you don't, I'm as good as dead. Morey had to lie about the time him and Tate tried to arrest me in my room. I talked to a guy on the phone, a guy here in town, and it was eleven o'clock then. Fifteen minutes later, no more, your highway patrolman picked me up ten miles south of town. Ask the motel manager what time Morey and Tate got the key to my room from him. Ask Glorieta. Ask her right now, Lieutenant, because you'll never get another chance to ask her again. Her doctor will see to that. Hendricks and Riker will see that he sees to it."

"This is ridiculous!" Hendricks burst out. "Lieutenant, this man is waking Mrs. Duncan. He's yelling so loud, he'd wake the dead."

"Like Tate?" Wilder snarled. "You wouldn't want that, though, would you, Hendricks? You handled that perfectly, didn't you? Who really killed Tate? The old man upstairs? Is he the one you're protecting?"

Hendricks's face grew almost purple. He closed his eyes a moment. His entire body swayed visibly. Forcing himself to appear calm, he turned to Bricken.

"Lieutenant, please have this man taken away before he causes Mrs. Duncan any worse anguish than he already has."

"That's right, Lieutenant," jeered Wilder mockingly. "Don't bother asking Mrs. Duncan how it happened. Just be very careful of all the anguish she's been through. Like when Tate was going over her back with a strap for old Duncan's kicks. That was before Tate decided he'd get in some kicks of his own. Look at her back! Don't take my word for it, Lieutenant. Look at her back."

"Shut up!" Hendricks screamed. "Stop that filthy mouth of yours!"

Hendricks lurched toward Wilder, his eyes blazing, his hands reaching out for Wilder's throat. Bricken jumped forward and got in front of Hendricks before he could take more than a couple of steps toward Wilder. Over Bricken's shoulder, Hendricks still stared bug-eyed at Wilder.

While Bricken tried to calm the man, Wilder turned his attention to Riker across the room, standing big and impassive near the corridor door.

One of the uniformed officers stepped forward to assist Bricken, but was waved away.

"It's alright, Officer," Bricken assured him. "Better wait outside. See if that doctor can get in here."

The cop left.

Bricken made certain Hendricks had gotten over his outburst before stepping back.

A couple of faces appeared in the doorway, peering in to see what all the noise was about. Impatiently, Bricken ordered the second uniformed officer, "Get them away from there. Shut that door."

"Hendricks, who are you covering for?" Wilder persisted. "Is it Riker?"

"Wilder, that's enough," Bricken cried. "Morey, I told you to get him out of here."

Wilder ignored him and went on talking, hammering away at Hendricks.

"Did Riker shoot Tate in the back while Tate was trying to slip it to Glorieta? Did you get your entire organization on the hop just to keep a quick gun like Riker safe from a murder rap?"

Morey grabbed Wilder's left arm. Wilder shook the hand off and slid away along the wall without taking his eyes off Hendricks.

Hendricks made a noise of some kind in his throat, but it didn't come out as words. He was shaking his head from side to side. "Stop this man, Bricken," he moaned. "Don't let him talk like that about her . . ."

Cursing under his breath, Bricken edged closer to Hendricks, ready to keep him from lunging for Wilder a second time.

Wilder flicked a quick glance toward Riker, who had stiffened. His eyes showed surprise. Now he tilted slightly forward onto the balls of his feet. His shoulders bunched as if he was getting ready to swing at someone. He stared at Wilder, then he swung his gaze to Morey, and finally to Hendricks.

Suddenly, something in the room had changed. Hendricks seemed to have lost his uncontrollable anger with remarkable swiftness. Turning his head, he stared thoughtfully at Riker.

Again, Morey took hold of Wilder's arm with his left hand, the one not holding the gun. Wilder let him. He didn't bother looking at Morey. It was Hendricks who had his full attention now.

Watching Hendricks's eyes, Wilder saw a strange expression in them as Hendricks thought over what had just been said.

Even Bricken was staring curiously at Hendricks when he noted how suddenly Hendricks had calmed down.

Hendricks stared across the room at Morey, then dropped his eyes to the gun in Morey's right hand. After a moment, he turned and stared at Riker, standing over near the corridor doorway.

"Is Riker the one, Hendricks?" Wilder asked softly, relentlessly. "Did he kill Tate?"

Bricken opened his mouth to say something, but didn't.

Instead, he went on watching the expression on Hendricks's face. Glancing over at Riker, he noticed how taut and ready the huge man appeared.

No one in the room spoke.

Footsteps could be heard out in the corridor as someone passed the closed door.

On the divan, Glorieta stirred, half-opened her eyes, stared at nothing for a sleepy moment, then closed her eyes once more.

"Did Riker do it?" Wilder pressed on remorselessly. "Hendricks, was Riker the one who shot Tate?"

Hendricks swung his head around and glanced at Wilder fleetingly, as if he was thinking over what Wilder had asked him. Then his glance rested on Morey and he kept it there.

Beside Wilder, Morey seemed to be having trouble swallowing. Wilder could hear his slight gulping sounds in the stretched out silence filling the room.

Suddenly, Hendricks turned and faced Riker.

Bricken was already squared away to Riker, a puzzled, watchful expression on his face.

"Yes," Hendricks croaked huskily. "Riker could have done it."

Three of them moved simultaneously. Both Riker and Bricken went for their guns, but Morey already had a gun in his hand.

Morey was the one Wilder was keeping an eye on.

Morey let go of Wilder's arm and raised his gun. He almost had Riker in his sights when Wilder slammed a fist into Morey's skull, just back of his eye.

Morey's weapon exploded a reflex shot, but it went into the ceiling: he was halfway to the floor before he tripped the trigger.

"Riker, don't shoot!" Wilder shouted. "Don't shoot. That's what Hendricks wants you to do."

Somehow, Riker heard.

He froze with his big semi-automatic only half-raised. Bricken had his service revolver all the way out, trained on Riker.

"He's correct, Mr. Riker," Bricken said softly. "Don't do any shooting. There's been enough of that."

After a long moment, Riker let out an endless breath and relaxed. Straightening a bit from his crouch, he looked around at everyone and chuckled.

"Sure, Lieutenant," he said quietly. "Like you say, no shooting. But let's hear some more of this guessing game, okay?"

"No more guessing," Wilder assured him. "I think that cinches it. Lieutenant, you don't have to bother with either of us — Riker or me. Hendricks must have killed Tate."

Riker nodded. "He did kill him."

Bricken kept his attention fixed on Riker.

"First, Mr. Riker," he said deliberately, "you had better hand across that cannon of yours. Then we'll think about sorting it all out."

Riker grinned, glanced contemptuously at Hendricks, hefted his handgun, shrugged, and flipped it into the air, catching it by the barrel. Walking over to Bricken, he handed him the weapon, butt-first.

"And here's Morey's service revolver, too, Lieutenant," Wilder said. "Hendricks gave good old Morey the go signal, and Morey was about to put a hole into Riker, as a favor to Hendricks."

For the first time, Bricken noticed Morey spread-eagled on his face at Wilder's feet. He came over, stared down at Morey's weapon lying on the floor nearby, and gave Wilder a quizzical glance as he bent and picked it up.

For a second, he stood there staring at Wilder. "You know," he mused aloud, "for the first time I'm beginning to think you may be on the level."

Wilder shrugged. "Lieutenant, I don't know Hendricks from a knothole," he said, "but from what I've seen of him in the last few minutes, I'd say he has some pretty strong feelings for Glorieta Duncan. Tate tried to rape her. She told me that. If Hendricks happened to walk in on that little scene, he may very well have grabbed the first thing he could reach and used it. Just so happened it turned out to be a gun."

Bricken wasn't convinced but he said thoughtfully, "Well, however it happened, we'll find out."

Hendricks was shaking his head in disbelief. "Lieutenant," he cried, "surely you can't believe that I would be capable of killing anyone . . . even someone like Tate . . ."

Wilder laughed.

"Even someone like Tate," he parroted.

A brief smile flickered across Riker's face.

Bricken didn't react at all. He simply said, quite courteously, "We'd best get into town, Mr. Hendricks. You come along too, Wilder. And you, Riker. We'll get all this squared away yet."

Bricken put a solicitous hand on Hendricks's arm.

Bewildered, Hendricks backed away from him. "But Lieutenant, I've got to stay here. I have to be here when Mrs. Duncan . . . she has no one to look after her . . ."

"Mrs. Duncan can come along with us," Wilder said. "We'll need her testimony, Mr. Hendricks. Don't forget, she saw you shoot Tate in the back just before she passed out. She told me you were the one who did the shooting."

Startled, Hendricks stared with frightened eyes at the woman lying asleep on the divan.

"She couldn't have seen," he protested angrily. "She was unconscious—"

Wilder burst out laughing. Even Riker chuckled aloud.

"There it is, Lieutenant," Wilder said cheerfully. Bricken nodded. He still wasn't smiling. As he accompanied Hendricks out into the corridor, he kept his hand on Hendricks's elbow and listened attentively to everything Hendricks was trying to tell him.

Wilder went over to the divan and stood gazing down at Glorieta, who was still deep in slumber. Strands of her black hair lay in long streaks across her face and hung limply down the front of her leather covered temporary bed.

The nurse moved closer and stood watching Wilder with a frown on her face.

"Looks like she slept through all of it," he observed. "Just as well."

"She must have been very tired," the woman said. "The sedative I gave her shouldn't have induced this deep a sleep."

"She was catching up," Wilder said.

He went over to Riker.

Before he could say anything, Riker growled, "Mister, you sure take big chances. You took one awhile ago, with me almost paying the bill for it."

"Riker, I was close enough to Morey to make sure he didn't get you," Wilder reminded him. "The rest? Well . . ." He shrugged. "All I could do about that was hope neither you nor Bricken would start shooting."

"I almost did," Riker said.

"Almost don't count," Wilder said, dismissing the matter.

"You'll be the one taking over around here, now that Hendricks is . . . going into retirement?"

"Could happen." Riker smiled.

"Do me a favor, will you, Riker? Get someone in the municipal building to sneak out the mug shots the cops took of me when they booked me for that assault rap the other night. And get my prints out too."

"Those are pretty impressive favors," Riker pointed out. "Now why would I do you a favor, even an easy one?"

"Maybe to show that you appreciate the way I just handed you this whole town on a platter?"

"I could have gotten it without you," Riker said negligently. "In fact, I been thinking of doing just that, for quite awhile."

Wilder grinned. "I thought you might have had something like that in mind," he said. "But there's still something else I can do for you, Riker, speaking of favors. I can butt out of this tank town by nightfall, if you get those things for me and clear up that phony assault rap they jailed me for. Plus maybe a little cash money, say ten G."

Riker roared with laughter. "This gets better and better. Ten thousand, is it? That's all? Wilder, why would I want you to get out of town? I like you. Stay around Thomaston as long as you want. You'll get to like the place."

"Yeah," Wilder said, grimacing, "the way I like wading in quicksand. You don't want me to move on? I thought maybe you might . . ."

"Nah, stay around as long as you like, Wilder." Without making a sound, Riker was laughing at him.

Wilder grinned back at him. "Okay," he responded. "I guess I'll have to make it real clear to you. Hendricks would have picked up on it long ago, what I'm selling here."

"Just what is it you are selling, Wilder? What would someone like you be selling that I would want to buy?"

"If I stay, I'll be staying with a playmate of mine."

Wilder glanced over at the divan. The nurse was fussing, trying to get a tiny pillow under Glorieta's head without waking her. Riker's eyes followed Wilder's glance.

"Mrs. Duncan likes me real good, I think," Wilder murmured. Riker wasn't smiling now. He watched Wilder's face, keeping his own expressionless.

"If I wanted her to get old Jeff Duncan committed or hospitalized, she'd jump at the chance. She'd be delighted to do it."

"If she can get the lawyers and judges to go along." Riker grinned.

"You've got a good point there," Wilder admitted. "Still, I'd be right beside her all the while she's trying, and neither you nor any of your muscle can scare me quite as quick as you might scare her . . . if she were alone, that is." He grinned at Riker disarmingly. "Not that you can't scare me too, Riker. Just that you can't scare me that fast. You beginning to read my message now?"

"You'll make trouble, is that it?"

"That's it. My way, you do me those little favors, and I get me some powder money, and the whole town's yours, including Glorieta Duncan. If you don't try bottling Glorieta-baby up too tight, maybe you won't have any trouble at all handling her. Depends how you work it, rough or smooth. Just make sure you don't start getting the hots for her, the way Hendricks did."

Two uniformed officers entered the room and went over to Morey, who was beginning to stir a little. They helped him sit up and half-carried him out into the hall and away.

Riker and Wilder stood aside, watching as they went past. Then Riker glanced at Wilder once more and nodded. "I'll see what I can do," he said.

"And isn't that all any of us can do?" Wilder asked. "Just see what we can do."

CHAPTER FOURTEEN

Wilder could have used a lot more than just five hours sleep, but five would have to do for the time being.

He was sitting in the afternoon sun on the south terrace wearing clothes he had found lain out in the room where he had done his sleeping. The clothes fit splendidly. He wondered how Glorieta could have gotten anyone to supply them so quickly.

She came out through the French door with his drink. The glass he had broken to get into the house had already been replaced. She stood beside him when he took the first swallow from the glass.

"Is it the way you like it?" she asked, when he brought the glass down from his mouth.

"Yeah," Wilder said. "Good stuff."

Her hand moved gently through his hair. When he looked up at her face, she seemed to react to his glance as if it had a tangible impact on her.

Wilder stared past her, down the immense sweep of lawn toward the lake and the water flowing like glass over the dam he had crawled across that morning.

A car turned off the county road, drove across the bridge, disappeared briefly into the belt of trees on this side, and came up the long drive to vanish toward the front of the house.

"That's probably those lawyers," Wilder observed.

"Will you come in with me? I'll feel better if you're there."

"Better if you handle it alone," he said. "You'll have to get used to doing these things without leaning on any more Hendrickses or Duncans or me's, or even Rikers." The ensuing silence became uncomfortable. He broke it by asking, "Did they take your husband away yet to the nursing home?"

She didn't say anything, just nodded.

"Good," he grunted. "Let the poor old guy die in his own time. The hell with all that life-support crap."

Her hand still rested against the back of his head, but it wasn't playing with his hair anymore. He kept staring into the distance until it became ridiculous. Then he looked up at her. Glorieta's eyes were dark and large and soft. Now her face was touched with sadness.

Wilder had all he could do to refrain from getting up and taking her in his arms and telling her the damn fool things that would make her feel good again, but which would lock him securely into her life here in yokelville.

"You're going away, aren't you." She said it, rather than asked it.

"I'm always going away, somewhere."

"I mean today," she persisted. "You aren't going to be here when I've finished with those lawyers, are you?"

"Maybe I'll be here." He detected the defensive tone in his voice and it annoyed him. "Maybe I'll take a stroll into the city, just to find out what it feels like when no cops or anyone else is looking for me to hang a killing-can on my tail." He grinned up at her, but her face remained serious and still looked sad.

The grin faded from Wilder's face.

Sharply, he added, "Don't ever count on me coming back anywhere, Glorieta."

Closing her eyes, she nodded. After a moment, she bent and kissed him softly on the lips. Then she straightened. "All right, Dan. I won't."

Turning, she went through the French door into the house.

Wilder returned his attention to his drink.

Another car was coming up the long drive. Wilder recognized Milo's Chevy and laughed. Apparently Riker had a sense of humor.

Finishing his drink quickly, Wilder walked along the side of the house to the front corner.

Milo was about to go up to the front door of the mansion when Wilder called him over.

There was a funny look on Milo's face as he approached.

Wilder watched him with amusement. Milo never quite met Wilder's gaze.

Hurriedly, Milo said, "Here's that stuff the cops took off you, Wilder — your wallet, and the other things. I told them I'd bring it to you out here . . ."

"I signed all of that out this morning," Wilder said evenly. "This is some other stuff."

"Oh." Milo looked down uncertainly at the envelope in his hand, then held it out. "Well, here it is."

Wilder took the envelope, but he kept staring at Milo without paying any attention to whatever was in it.

"You crossed me the other night, Milo, but good."

Milo fell back a step. Now his wide eyes looked directly at Wilder. "Wilder, I had to," he whispered. "I had to. What'd you expect me to do, sit still while you went blasting all over town in my car? I just told the fuzz it got stole. And the license—"

"No, that wasn't all, Milo," Wilder interrupted. "You gave out a list of places I'd be likely to go. They wouldn't have picked up that load of yours nearly as quick as they did if you hadn't rattled off the whole string of addresses I got from your lousy phone book. First Morey, then Hendricks, and even Duncan." He shook his head, staring coldly at Milo, who stood there with his head bent taking it. "Uh-uh, Milo," he went on. "You turned me over and in spades. There's no other way to look at it."

Milo tried to think of something to say, but when he finally did, it never came to much.

Wilder ignored it, anyway. He didn't even listen. He kept studying Milo, then he glanced down at the envelope Milo had brought. Tearing off one end, he squinted inside and smiled.

Milo watched, curious.

"What's in it, Wilder?"

"Nothing, Milo. Get in your heap. Drive me into town."

Wilder didn't look back at the Duncan mansion piled up at the crown of the gentle slope above the southern tip of the lake. He was too busy making a production of getting the pictures and the negatives of his mug shots out of the envelope, and the card with his fingerprints on it.

He had no way of knowing whether they had already sent copies of the prints on to Washington, but maybe they hadn't. He hoped they hadn't.

Putting all of it inside the jacket of his new suit, he waited until Milo had driven the Chevy through quiet neighborhoods and was working his way into Thomaston's Saturday afternoon traffic tie-ups before he pulled the money out of the envelope.

Milo's head snapped around at the sight of the packet of bills.

Slowly, Wilder began counting the money. "Eight thousand . . . nine . . . nine-five . . . nine-six . . . nine-seven . . . nine-eight . . .nine-nine . . . twenty, forty, sixty, seventy, eighty, ninety, ten thousand even. Okay, Municipality of Thomaston and all your freedom loving citizens, we're quits. Milo, you can drop me off over there at the bus station."

Milo licked his lips. He was sweating. His eyes slid sideward to watch as Wilder put the loot away.

"You ain't gonna pull that job?" he asked. "That heist I had lined up. You could do it easy, Wilder, now the heat's off you. Next Friday night—"

Wilder watched him, keeping a straight face, but his eyes were laughing. "No, Milo. I don't need the dough, not anymore. I've got a stake again. You better get someone else for that job. Turn him in too, if things go wrong. Milo-boy, you're too rich for my blood."

The Chevy pulled to a stop. Traffic in the sun-drenched street was at a standstill, halted by a stoplight ahead, at the bus depot's corner.

Opening the door on his side of the car, Wilder got out. He slammed the door shut and, grinning, took one last satisfying look at Milo's lugubrious face before turning away and threading his way through the stopped cars and trucks to the sidewalk.

Before he reached the entrance of the bus station, the traffic started to move again.

A car pulled into the curb beside Wilder. For a second, he thought it might be Milo, still trying, but when he took a look, it wasn't Milo's Chevy. It was a convertible with a woman at the wheel. He kept going along the sidewalk toward the entrance to the terminal.

A woman's voice called, "Wilder."

Turning, he looked around to see who had called.

"Over here, Wilder."

The woman in the convertible was waving to attract his attention. After a moment's uncertainty, Wilder recognized her. He went over.

"Hi, Marge." He noted her luggage piled in back. "Leaving good old Thomaston?"

She smiled wryly but her nod was emphatic. "Yes, and for keeps. I draw the line when someone like Riker takes charge. Things never seem to go too smoothly under the Rikers."

"Maybe you're doing the smart thing," he agreed. "Which way are you headed?"

"What difference does it make? Want to come along? I'm . . . a little lonesome. I've been here in Thomaston a lot longer than I usually stay anywhere."

Wilder hesitated, watching her, thinking over the offer. When she noticed his hesitation, her eyes snapped and she said crisply, "You don't have to, if you don't want to."

"No, no, it isn't that," Wilder assured her. "It's only that I've just wrapped things up with one of the always girls. I don't want to get mixed up with another."

"Always girls?" She squinted up at him, her hand shielding her eyes from the afternoon sun. Beyond her, the traffic passed ceaselessly. Along the sidewalk, pedestrians ambled and strolled and scurried in the Saturday afternoon heat and sunshine. "Always . . . you mean Glorieta?" Marge asked.

"Yeah. She's one of the ones who never know that always is only three weeks long, if that. Like them."

He tilted his head toward the people passing, hot and sticky and happy and quarrelsome, waiting for evening to come so it would be cool again. And when it came, they would start waiting for tomorrow, so the sun would be shining again.

"The always people," he grinned mockingly. "They don't know, either."

When he stopped and didn't continue, Marge frowned. "Know what?" she asked. "Wilder, what are you talking about?"

"That tomorrow is right now," he explained. "And yesterday . . .?" He grinned and shrugged. "Yesterday was a thousand years ago."

Marge sat watching him, and then she observed the people walking both ways along the sidewalk fronting the bus station. "What a grim picture!" she murmured. "Anyway, don't worry about me, Wilder. I'm not one of your always girls. Three weeks is twice as long as people like you and I could possibly stay together."

He grinned. "I didn't think you were one of them, Marge. Okay, I'll come along for the ride and the laughs. But with one condition."

"What condition is that?" she asked, her eyes narrowing, watching him suspiciously. "Always be wary of a man with conditions."

"That you promise not to take the highway south out of town," he specified. "Every time I get down that way, I land in all kinds of trouble."

Marge threw her head back and laughed. "All right, big boy. We'll take another road out of town. Happy now?"

"Yeah. Be right back."

He went into the bus station, got his carry-on bag from the locker he'd stashed it in that morning, and went back outside. Stuffing the bag in among her things in back, he slid in beside Marge and they took off.

Within fifteen minutes, they had left the summer afternoon heat of the town behind and were cutting east on the interstate.

Their always time together might turn out to be three days or three weeks or three months, but when it ended, all it would add up to was just another string of yesterdays for each of them to remember.

Or not.

Chris O'Grady is the author of numerous short stories and novels. He lives in Hampstead, North Carolina.

Twit Publishing

Dallas-based. Indie. Fiction. Awesome.

Want to find out more about Twit Publishing?

Then go to www.TwitPublishing.com

Read about the company, hear about upcoming releases, and find links to our authors.

* * * * * * *

You can also find us at:

www.Facebook.com/TwitPublishing

www.TwitPublishing.WordPress.com

and

www.Twitter.com/TwitPublishing

www.ingramcontent.com/pod-product-compliance
Lightning Source LLC
LaVergne TN
LVHW090950080826
845145LV00003B/960

* 9 7 8 0 9 8 4 5 4 7 7 8 4 *